Wrapped In His Thug Luv

For The Holiday

By: Ro.J

Prologue

Remember having those ladies' nights and you and your girls getting drunk having conversations about how your home girl was stupid because she let her nigga do this or do that? Ever notice the main one giving advice be the main one who was the dumbest and main one whose nigga was probably the one dogging her ass out? If you didn't notice, it's probably because you are probably exactly who I'm talking about. How do I know? I was that same girl.

The only difference is I was young and didn't have a clue about love and how a man was really supposed to treat you! I thought as long as yo nigga was keeping you fly and keeping your pockets laced, then he was the best nigga in the world. I was definitely all the way wrong.

So, sit back, relax and grab a blunt, a drink or whatever it is that you do to relax and let me tell you my story. I hope you learn some shit because this shit happens every day to some females who mistake lust for love. Love does not hurt and it damn sure don't make you forget the person you are. It definitely shouldn't put your ass behind bars for some shit you didn't do. I mean it's cool to be a ride a die for a nigga, but would that nigga do the same for you?

They say when somebody shows you their true colors, believe it. I mean I saw the warning signs. I just didn't want to believe them. Let me quit preaching and get to my story. I rode for a nigga that didn't give two fucks about me. I thought I was doing the right thing by sticking by my so-called nigga. Meanwhile the whole time I was riding for him, he was out here making me look like a damn fool. So, sit back and let me tell you my story. My nightmare started the summer before my senior year.

Chapter One

Rhae

Growing up, I can't say I had a bad childhood because I didn't. I was raised by my mama and she busted her ass working two jobs to provide for me and my sisters. I had no clue where my deadbeat ass daddy was because he left when I was about thirteen after my youngest sister Peaches was born. We stayed in a decent neighborhood and never missed a meal. I just did dumb shit for no apparent reason at all.

One thing I did learn was you had to have both book and street smarts to make it out here in this cold world, and if you are looking for something to be handed to you because of your looks, then you definitely needed to reevaluate life because that way of thinking would have you fucked up and lonely or in a situation you couldn't get yourself out of like me.

I met my first love, or should I say my first heartache Za'Kari, on Belle Isle, which was a local beach that was on an island in downtown Detroit where all the dope boys and wannabes hung out. This was exactly where all of the hood rats came with hopes of some dope boy snatching them up and taking them up out the hood.

It was your typical hot summer day, and everybody was parked by the water relaxing. Some were drinking, smoking, shooting dice, or just standing around talking shit. My right hand Kazie and I decided that we were going to walk to the other side of the beach because it seemed like the water was cleaner over there. While crossing the street, I locked eyes with the finest nigga I've ever seen in my whole eighteen years on this earth.

He definitely could be bae. He was standing about six foot three, with caramel skin and tattoos all over his body with long pretty dreads that he wore down his back, and whew, I'm not going to even describe how big his dick print was in the basketball shorts he wore. He had pretty straight white teeth with dimples. Now I usually stayed away from guys like him because I wasn't the type of female to be fighting over some nigga that was supposed to be mine and plus my mom wasn't having that shit at all. But the way he was looking, I was willing to take a risk today.

Za'Kari stared at me the whole time I walked across the street. I didn't want to seem desperate, so I just kept walking. I knew he was staring at my ass because that's what most niggas did when it came to me and my right hand Kazie. I stood five foot six, weighing in at about one hundred seventy-five pounds, with smooth caramel skin. I was addicted to tattoos, so I had a few. I had long hair that passed my shoulders that I usually wore bone straight with a part down the middle. I didn't wear make-up because I didn't have the patience to put it on. It was too damn hot anyway. That shit would have been gone as soon as I applied it.

"Bitch you got us out here on our hoe stroll and it's hot as hell." Kazie said while popping her gum.

I just shook my head because Kazie stayed complaining about something, but I was used to it because that was just her.

"I know right. I'm glad my ass don't wear makeup because I would have sweat that shit off. Let's go sit over there and put our feet in the water." I said while pointing towards the lake.

"Uh no bitch. You can't put yo feet in that contaminated water. We are in Detroit, not somewhere like Miami where you can see through the water." Kazie replied while still walking towards the lake.

"Girl shut up. Don't act like you ain't never put your feet in no Detroit water. You wash your ass in it, and even Miami has dirty water. Now bring yo high sadity ass on and stop being petty." I said while walking and eyeing the group of fellas standing by their cars smoking and shooting dice.

I guess Za'Kari got tired of staring and decided to come speak. His voice was like music to my ears.

"Damn little mama. Let me walk with you". Za'Kari said while walking towards me. I wanted to run and jump in his arms and tell his ass we didn't have to go anywhere, but I didn't want to look desperate and thirsty.

"I'm not going nowhere, but over there by the lake It's hot as hell out here but it's a free country. You can go wherever you like." I said while continuing to walk past him.

"Yeah I agree it's hotter than a motherfucka out here, so I think I will go sit by the lake wit yo sexy ass." Za'Kari said while grabbing my arm so he could walk beside me.

I swear I drooled when he stopped to take off his shirt, because his body was beautiful. He had a million tattoos and had just enough muscle to pick my thick ass up. I swear every time his ass got closer to me, the wetter my pussy got. There was another guy walking with him, and he was just as fine. I figured it was his brother because they looked alike. The only difference was he was a little darker and his hair was cut to perfection and he had a beard that was perfectly lined up. To be honest, I would talk to either one of them. I knew Kazie's hot in ass was feeling him too because she kept looking at him smiling and licking her lips. But he wasn't really paying her no attention because he was too busy mugging his brother like he pissed him off or something.

"I am not about to be the third wheel. That's lame as hell Rhae Rhae." Kazie said while interrupting our conversation. I knew that was coming because no one was really paying her no mind and she didn't like being ignored. I don't know why she thought that she would be the third wheel when this fine ass nigga were sitting right here in her face. Shit, she better shoot her shot before one of these hood rats snatch his ass up.

"How are you the third wheel when I don't know these niggas? We just chilling. Plus we about to smoke." I replied while reaching in my bra and pulling a rolled blunt out.

"Plus Lil Mama my big brother Zaylen can keep you company." Za'Kari said while pointing to his brother.

She looked up at Zaylen and started smiling, looking so desperate. I just shook my head. I don't know how many times I had to tell this heifer that we don't chase niggas, niggas chase us. He really didn't look like he wanted to be bothered with her, but he was just doing it just because she was here and so was he. To be honest he kept staring at me. I don't know what that was about, but Za'Kari had all my attention. I hope he didn't think I was hoe because I was far from that. Little did I know, I should have been paying attention to Zaylen the whole time.

Chapter Two

Rhae

Let's fast forward six months no need to go through all the shit I been through with Za'Kari's ass from the STDs, to the knocking his side bitches out on the regular because they wanted to test me. This fool didn't even respect me enough to go home at a decent hour, yet here I am.

I woke up from the sound of my alarm. Damn it was my last week of class before I graduated. I hope Za'Kari was not late picking me up this morning because once Ms. Johnson close her door, I couldn't take my final in advanced English and I needed this class to graduate. I reached for my iPhone to dial his number.

"Hello," Za'Kari answered.

"Za'Kari are you awake, bae? I gotta be on time because it's my finals today." I replied while getting out of bed.

"Damn Rhae Rhae, a nigga just went to sleep. I'm on my way. You better be ready to cause a nigga tired as hell." Zakarri said while yawning into the phone.

"Well if yo ass would have brought me a car, we wouldn't have to worry about you picking me up." I replied while looking in my closet for something to wear.

"No correction if yo ass would get off yo ass and get yo own money instead of spending mine, you would have a car. Now get the fuck off my line I'll be there in a minute." Za'Kari yelled into the phone.

"Damn Za'Kari who are you talking too? Go back to sleep." Some girl said in the background.

The phone went silent and this nigga hung up. I know this nigga was not just laid up with some thot ass bitch. I swear the bitch sounded like Kazie. Nah I was tripping. I know she wouldn't do that to me knowing how I feel about Za'Kari. Plus she was as loyal as they come.

I had to hurry up and get dressed because I didn't want to be late, but you best believe as soon as I get in the car, I'm going to be like one of those detectives on *The First 48*, interrogating his cheating ass. Since I was only going to be in school a few hours, I decided to keep it simple. I got in the shower and washed up with my favorite body wash and got out. I brushed my teeth and rinsed my mouth with mouthwash.

I decided to put on some leggings with my senior shirt with a fresh pair of Jordan 12s to complete my outfit. I grabbed my hairbrush and my Ebin edge control and put my hair in a high ponytail. I looked at myself in the mirror and of course as always, I was looking good. One thing mama taught us, was as ladies, you always take care of your hygiene and always step out looking like something, because first impressions are everything. On the way out, I grabbed my diamond hoop earrings and my mac lip gloss and I headed downstairs.

"Good morning loves." I said while grabbing a piece of bacon off my little sister Passion's plate.

My mom had cooked us breakfast and was sitting in her favorite chair watching Fox 2 news.

"Good morning pumpkin. You had another package come from FedEx this morning. That's the fifth one this week." My mom said while never taking her eyes off the TV.

"I know Ma. Za'Kari does a lot of online shopping and he sends it here because someone is always home." I replied while rolling my eyes.

I loved my mommy to death but sometimes she could be irritating as hell. She always had something to say. I mean damn, I was eighteen yet she treated me like I was twelve. I know Za'Kari would never have me doing anything that would hurt me he loves me.

"Okay Rhae Rhae, please don't be getting yourself caught up in no illegal shit over a nigga that can give two fucks about you." My mom replied while getting up and putting her plate in the sink.

"Ma what are you talking about? Za'Kari would never have me doing anything illegal. He loves me." I said while kissing her on her cheek.

"Rhae what do you know about love? You are only eighteen but talking to you is like talking to a brick wall. Just remember a hard head gon' make a soft ass." My mom said while shaking her head.

"I hear you Ma." I said while grabbing my book bag.

There was no need to try to plead my case because I would never win. I kissed my mom on the cheek again and ran out the door because this nigga was blowing the horn like I lived outdoors.

"Za'Kari why do you insist on being an asshole every day? And what bitch was you laid up with last night? Don't fucking lie either." I said while slamming the car door.

"Rhae, it's too fucking early for all this nagging and shit. That was my fucking cousin. I keep telling yo ass, you my girl and not my fucking mama. I'm a grown ass man and when you realize that shit, the better off we will be. Keep on and yo ass gone be replaced. Now just sit back and shut the fuck up." Za'Kari said while pulling off down the street.

"Tuh. Replaced by who? Ain't no bitch gonna ride for yo dumb ass like me nigga. Let's not forget what the fuck I do for you. If anybody gone be replaced it's gone be yo ass and you shut the fuck up." I yelled while pushing his head with my finger.

Next thing you know this nigga back handed me something serious. The nigga hit me so hard, my head hit the window.

"See what the fuck you made me do? You don't have to remind me what the fuck you do for me because the shit you doing for me, keep yo pockets fat and the latest clothes on yo fat ass. You get on my motherfuckin' nerves. Yeah, I was laid up wit a bitch and guess what? I'm about to go back and lay up under that bitch and get me some more pussy. Now what you gon do? Exactly what I thought, absolutely nothing. Now take yo fat ass in that school and take yo exam and I'll be here to pick you up and let me see one of these punks sniffing around my pussy, I'm fucking you and him up. Now get the fuck out." Za'Kari yelled while parking in front of the school.

Oh I swear to God, I wanted to punch this bitch in the throat. Here I am risking me and my family's life for some nigga who don't even respect my dumb ass. I know we hate listening to our parents, but I swear to God I wish I would have listened to my mama.

Now I'm in this shit too deep and I can't get out of it. If I send the shit back, he's gon' kill me. If I tell the police, he's gon' kill me. Either way, I'm fucked! This shit wasn't even worth it. I'm in love with a straight up fuck boy!

You are not going to get caught bae. It's just a couple of packages bae, was all I could hear in my head while I walked towards my class. Why didn't he have the shit delivered to that bitches house since he was about to go lay up with her. I was not about to continue to let this nigga play me.

When I get out of school, I was just going to give him all his shit and tell him to get the hell on.

I walked to Kazie's locker to meet her. This was our everyday routine when her crazy ass did come to school. To be honest, I don't think she had enough credits to graduate. I tried to keep her on the right track, but Kazie wasn't as blessed as me to have someone who cared about her wellbeing. Her mom had her at a young age and she acted more like her friend then her parent. Hell Kazie even smoked and drank with her mama Julissa. Well one thing was for sho', Brenda Faye was not playing that shit at all, and to be honest, I know I don't want no smoke.

I decided to call Kazie and see where she was, because we literally had five minutes to get to class.

"Hey Rhae. I'm not coming to school today. I'm tired plus I stayed out late last night wit my new boo. I didn't study last night anyway and I'm not graduating anyway so why even waste my time." Kazie said while rolling a blunt.

"Girl I don't even know why I even try with you. You know damn well you could just take your exams and just go to summer school. It's more to life than getting high and hanging out wit those broke ass niggas in the hood. But it's your life do you boo." I replied while walking towards class.

"Rhae don't judge me like you ain't out here chasing behind Za'Kari's no good ass. It's been plenty nights we were out late looking for his ass. So, bitch don't judge me." Kazie said while hanging up the phone.

"Bae who you talking too?" The male said in the background.

I swear to God that nigga in the background sounded just like Za'Kari's ass. Let me find out the bitch he had been laying up with is my best friend. I swear to God it's going to be a lot of slow singing and flower bringing for both of their asses.

Chapter Three

Kazie

Rhae was always trying to lecture somebody like her shit was all the way together. I mean yeah, she was my best friend, but I really didn't like her because to me, she always thought that she was better than me. The only thing that Rhae had over me was that she had a mother that actually gave a fuck about her. My mother had me at a young age and let's just say, she had no clue about how to be a parent. I know there is no book on how to be a parent, but damn. It's just some things that were common sense. What parent makes their child pay rent at fifteen? I know what parent, my parent. I had to pay my mother two hundred dollars a month or be out on the streets with the crackheads and homeless people. So, to avoid that, I did the only thing I knew how to do, and that was give these hood niggas this WAP and get that cash, while working part-time at Wal-Mart. I mean it was not something that I enjoyed doing but I was out here by myself trying to survive. It was a dog eat dog world out here.

I wish I did have a mother like Mrs. Brenda, because she busted her ass for her girls, and she made sure they were straight. Rhae stayed in the latest clothes and shoes and all she had to do was go to school and take care of her little sisters. Simple right? My life was anything but. One thing I had over her was I wasn't out here being played by no nigga because I never caught feelings. She was so caught up in this nigga that her dumb ass allowed him to send drugs to her house, knowing if Mrs. Brenda found out, she would kill her ass. She's risking her freedom for a nigga that is out here fucking anything with a pussy between their legs. I know because I am one of the bitches he's fucking. Once again don't blame me, blame your mammy. Shit Za'Kari is how I pay my mama's rent and my high ass Verizon bill. Plus, I ain't gone even lie he did have that dope dick.

Za'Kari and I been fucking around just as long as he had been with Rhae. One day he came over to my house looking for Rhae, so he claimed and he was drunk and high off weed and an E pill. One thing led to another and the next thing I know, he had my ass bent over in the kitchen giving me back shots. Once he started lacing my pockets, I started getting possessive over him because I wanted him to give me all the money. At first, I was just playing my role as the side chick, but when he stood me up a few times for her, it made me feel some type of way.

So, I put my plan into motion to become the main chick. I did everything that nigga asked me to do including sucking and fucking him wherever and whenever. She better go and holla at Zaylen's lame ass. He got that dope dick too. He just was not my type I liked a thug and he was more of a corporate thug, plus he was not feeling me at all. I think that he had something for Rhae, because he never had been really into me unless he was gay.

I had been trying to get pregnant by Za'Kari so that he could leave Rhae's ass alone. You see, if I had his baby, then he has no choice but to take care of me for the rest of my life. I was not made to work because of my fucked-up attitude. I had been fired from all the jobs I've worked because I got into some kind of altercation with my coworkers or supervisor. So, a bitch got to do what I got to do to secure the bag.

So, here I am sitting in the bathroom with three pregnancy tests reading the directions so I can see if my plan was successful. I peed on all three sticks and placed them on the paper towel I had on the sink. I swear this was the longest sixty seconds of my life. The anticipation was killing me. When those two blue lines showed up on all three sticks I started jumping up and down because now Za'Kari's ass was stuck.

I opened the door and ran and jumped on the bed where Za'Kari was.

"Damn Kaz why would you come and jump on the bed like that a nigga trying to get some sleep." Za'Kari yelled while putting the pillow over his head.

"Za'Kari you need to wake up. I got something to tell you bae!" I said while pulling the pillow off his head.

"Kaz whatever the fuck it is, it can wait till I wake up. I only got a few hours before I got to go pick up Rhae from school. Damn I can't never get no sleep. I'm gone start taking my ass home." Za'Kari mumbled while turning back over getting comfortable.

See what I'm saying? This bitch Rhae was always in my fucking way. How the fuck you laid up in my bed thinking about another bitch? I know damn well she's not fucking him better than I am, because this nigga wouldn't be laid up in my bed every fucking night. I wonder how the heifer going to feel when she found out I'm pregnant by her so-called nigga. I smiled because I couldn't wait to crush her little heart and feelings.

I threw the pregnancy test and hit him in the forehead because he had just pissed me off with his last statement. He opened his eyes to see what hit him in his big ass forehead. He sat up and grabbed the test off the bed and looked at me.

"What the fuck is this Kaz?"

"Come on Za'Kari, don't tell me you don't know what a pregnancy test looks like. Congratulations nigga we pregnant!" I yelled.

"Wait what how when I strapped up every time?"

"What do you mean how? A condom only protects about 85% of woman from getting pregnant so umm yeah like I said we pregnant."

"Damn this some straight up bullshit. I mean I rock with you I really do. But this is not a good time for us to bring a kid into this world. I am with your best friend. How you think she gon' feel?"

I had to count to ten before I spazzed out on this nigga.

"I don't give a fuck how she feels at this point. I mean you wasn't thinking about how the fuck she would feel when you was fucking the shit out of me. Now you want to care about her feelings? I am not aborting my baby, so u better figure out what the fuck you gon' tell her or I'll tell her. It really don't matter to me." I yelled because he was pissing me off.

"Now I was trying to be fucking considerate about your feelings, but since you call yourself being in savage mode, let me tell yo dumb ass what you gon' do. You gone take this two hundred dollars and make that appointment and get a fucking abortion or be a single fucking parent." Za'Kari yelled while throwing money everywhere.

Well that didn't go as planned. What the fuck is wrong with me? I can never win. It's like I was cursed at birth or something. I swear to God I wish something would happen to Rhae where her ass would go away for a while so that Za'Kari would see that I'm the one he needs to be with. I decided to roll me up one because I needed to think about a way to get her ass up out of here. I don't know why but I swear I think better when I'm high.

After smoking a blunt and drinking a couple of cups of weed Kool-Aid, my mind was all over the place. The only solution I could come up with was hollering at my auntie who worked in narcotics for the Detroit Police Department. She was always looking for a good lead so she could get that good promotion. I figured I would just tell her about how Rhae's dumb ass has pounds of weed delivered to her house a couple of days out the week. I scrolled through my iPhone until I came across my auntie Tish's number. One thing my mama did teach me is go after what you want and that's exactly what I was about to do, starting with this phone call.

"Hello this is Detective Brown. How can I help you?"

"Hey auntie Tish. You got a minute? I have some valuable information that I think you can use."

"What type of information Kaz and make it quick because I have a meeting with the captain in ten minutes." Damn she got an attitude. If telling her this information didn't benefit me, I would have just hung up on her ass.

"Okay I'll make it quick. Well this girl that I hang out with sometimes has a boyfriend who is a drug dealer and he has packages shipped to her house via FedEx. It's a lot of drugs."

"Mmm oh really and what's this so-called friend's name?"

"Her name is Rhaelyn Steele." I said without hesitation.

"Oh, we have already been watching her. Thanks for that confirmation. Now I can get the warrant I needed. You wouldn't mind testifying in court, would you?" My Auntie Tish asked.

"Whoa. whoa. Can't this be like an anonymous tip? I don't want to be labeled as no snitch around the hood."

"You young people be killing me with this snitching shit. Nobody is above the law, but I'll make sure no one knows you gave me this valuable information."

I didn't give a fuck what she was talking about. Nobody wanted to be known as a snitch. None of the hood niggas would give me the time of day and that's how I make my money. I hope she sent Rhae's ass away for a long time.

Chapter Four

Rhae

I walked through the halls hoping my face wasn't fucked up because I was definitely not in the fucking mood to be explaining shit to nobody. I made it to Ms. Johnson's class just in time. The bitch seen me walking up the hall and closed the door. She could have waited. I swear everybody was getting on my fucking nerves today.

"Ms. Steele, you're lucky I feel like being nice. You know once my door is closed that means you are late, and that means you can't take the final. Now hurry up and have a seat." Ms. Johnson said while rolling her eyes.

The bitch passed out our exam and everybody got to work. An hour into the exam, there was a knock at the classroom door. Our principal Mr. Evans walked in and whispered in Ms. Johnson's ear. She looked dead at me and shook her head. *What the fuck was that about* I wondered.

"Ms. Steele, go with Mr. Evans please." Ms. Johnson replied while pointing to the door.

"But I'm not finished." I said while pointing to my exam.

"You can finish when you return. Now please gather your things and let's go." Mr. Evans replied while walking towards the door.

I gathered my stuff and left out of the class. As I was walking to the office, all type of crazy shit was going through my brain. When I walked in, I saw two detectives waiting at the door.

"Ms. Steele, I am Detective Brown and this is my partner, Detective Thomas." Detective Brown said while pointing to the other Detective.

"Ok and you are here for what? I have a final exam that I was taking. Are my mom and sisters okay?" I asked with a worried look on my face.

"Yes, everything is fine with your mom and sisters. We are going to need you to come with us down to the station." Detective Brown replied.

"What wait? Don't my mom have to be with me in order for y'all to question me?" I asked not moving.

"Technically no because you're eighteen and by law, you are an adult now. Do you wanna leave now willingly, or do you want to have your friends see you leaving here with handcuffs?" Detective Thomas said while swinging his handcuffs.

"I guess I'll go, but I haven't done anything so it will be a waste of time." I replied with all the confidence I could. Because lord knows I was scared as hell.

"That's what they all say. Let's go." Detective Brown said while shaking her head with disappointment.

I followed them outside to the police car. They didn't put me in handcuffs, so I pulled my phone out and texted Za'Kari.

Me: Aye Bae we have to cancel our date something came up. Looks like I will be tied up for a minute I'll call once I'm done.

Bae: wrong number.

Instead of taking me straight downtown, the officers did a detour and took me to my house. When I pulled up to my house, it looked like some shit off *The First 48*. Police cars were everywhere, and the nosey ass neighbors were outside looking. They let me out of the back of the police car and guided me in the house.

"Now usually we don't do this, but before we take you downtown, I wanted to show you how much trouble you are in young lady." Detective Thomas said while walking behind me.

The door had been kicked in and my mama's house was torn up. I mean shit was everywhere. I walked straight back to my room, forgetting that the two detectives were with me. When I made it to my room and went to the closet, the safe I kept all Za'Kari's weed and coke in was gone. Now I am far from a drug dealer, but I am smart enough to know it was enough to sit my ass down for a while. Only thing I could do is think about the conversation me and mama had this morning. Only thing I could do was cry. Tears started rolling down my face instantly.

"Is there anything you would like to tell us because as you can see, we already got what we came looking for. We have been watching you for a while now and we know you have nothing to do with the drugs, and we also know Za'Kari is your boyfriend." Detective Thomas said while shaking his head.

"Like I said I don't know what you are talking about." I said while wiping the tears from my face.

"So, let me get this shit straight. You don't know nothing about the safe that was in your closet in your room? Why are you sitting here crying. Only guilty people cry! Now where did the drugs come from Rhae?" Detective Thomas said while pointing to the empty space in my closet.

"I said I don't know what you are talking about." I said while trying to walk out of my room.

"What the hell is going on in here and look at my fucking house! Some damn body got some explaining to do." My mama yelled while walking into our house with my two little sisters.

Only thing I could do is put my head down, because I already was in some deep shit, and I couldn't take the look of disappointment and hurt on my mama's face. I didn't even want to look at my little sister's face because I couldn't imagine what was going through their heads. All this for a nigga who couldn't even be a man an own up to his shit. Mama was right, a hard head makes a soft ass because right now I was feeling like I was fucked.

"We have a warrant, Ms. Steele. Ask your daughter what's going on because she definitely not talking to us. Maybe you can talk some sense into her. We will give you a few moments with her, but she is definitely going with us." Detective Thomas said while walking out of my room and closing the door.

"Rhae, please tell me that dumb ass nigga of yours was not stashing drugs in my damn house. Did I not teach you better than that? I know you not that fucking dumb. I knew it was something suspicious about those damn packages, but me thinking I raised you right and trusting you, I didn't open them. That's my fuck up as a parent. Where did I go wrong? Let me guess now he is nowhere to be found? I told you, you don't know shit about love. Somebody who loves you won't put you in harm's way or do anything to jeopardize your freedom. Where am I going to get money for you a damn lawyer? You didn't think about none of that shit when you were being a rider for his no good ass. You young girls make me sick. Just let these little bum ass, fake ass dope boys tell you anything. Get the fuck out my face before I kill your dumb ass. I'll follow you to the station." My mama said with tears in her eyes.

She didn't have to tell me twice. At this point I would rather go with the detectives. They still didn't put me in handcuffs, which I was thankful for because I needed to get in contact with Za'Kari's ass. I am not going down for this shit. I ain't no fucking snitch either. I don't know what the hell I'm going to do. I used to think I was grown but now I see I really didn't have a clue about life love or none of that shit. Only thing I wanted to do was to go home. I tried texting Za'Kari again and got the same *wrong number* response.

Man, what the fuck this nigga mean wrong number? He better come up with a way to get me out this shit. I texted Kazie next because I needed her to try and call his ass.

Me: on my way downtown call Za'Kari 313 224 9990 and let him know it's all bad and I will call him later can't go into detail right now on my way to the police station on Nevada.

Bestie: Damn Rhae ok calling now what the fuck you mean you on your way to the police station what the fuck going on?

We got to the police station on Nevada in no time. It was so quick I couldn't even get my thoughts together. Damn, I'm glad they weren't taking me downtown. Oh well hopefully my mom is right behind us because I didn't want to deal with these bastards by myself. I got out of the patrol car and they walked me into what I am assuming was the interrogation room.

"So, Ms. Steele, do you know why you are here?" Detective Brown asked.

"Ah no and I wish you would tell me." I said while rolling my eyes.

"See we have been watching you for a while and we know that you have FedEx packages delivered to your house at least five times a week. We know there were a lot of drugs delivered to your house. Now whose drugs are they?" Detective Thomas asked.

"I do a lot of online shopping. I don't know what drugs you are talking about." I answered.

"I already see how this is going to go. Let me guess Za'Kari Walker is your boyfriend and you had no clue it was drugs in those packages? So, they just mysteriously got sent to your house? You know I've been a detective for many years, so it ain't too much bullshit that you can get pass me, right? And we got an anonymous tip that you have had drugs delivered to your house. So, are you going to stop lying now?" Detective Thomas said while hitting his hand on the table.

"I don't know what you are talking about. I'm not the only person that lives in that house and Za'Kari has nothing to do with packages that come to my house. He has his own house that packages can go to." I said while leaning back in my chair.

"So are you saying that those are you and your mom packages because I know damn well your little sisters wouldn't have packages coming to the house." Detective Brown yelled.

"Like I said, I have no idea what you are talking about so whatever you are assuming it's not true." I yelled back because I was getting frustrated with them asking me the same damn questions.

"So, you are really sitting up here all alone, while Mr. Walker laying up with the next bitch, while telling us that he has nothing to do with the packages of drugs being sent to your home?" Detective Thomas asked while shaking his head.

"What drugs?" I asked.

"I see you think this is a fucking game little girl. Did you forget we raided your home this morning and we retrieved a lot of drugs that could put you away for a very long time? You will be locked up for years while Mr. Walker is a free man, not thinking twice about your dumb ass." Detective Brown said while laughing.

"Like I said I don't know what you are talking about. Can I see my mom?" I asked.

"Yes, you can see her this is going to be the last time you get to talk to her or your siblings because you're going to jail for a long time. You worked so hard to graduate and you won't even make it because you won't tell the truth. Look sweetheart, we know your whole story. You are a good kid and you have your whole life ahead of you. If we were to bring Mr. Walker here right now, what do you think he would say? All the evidence points toward you." Detective Thomas said.

"Can I see my family now?" I asked while looking towards the door.

He looked at me, shook his head and walked out the room and slammed the door. I felt like the walls were closing in on me. For some reason, all I could think about was the conversation me and my mama had this morning.

I had been sitting in this room for a good thirty minutes and they still hadn't let my mom come back here to talk to me. The more time went by, the angrier I got. How could I be so stupid to let a no good as nigga put me in a position that I can't get out of? I don't know shit about selling drugs, so why am I here again? All of these questions were going through my head, and finally the door opened, and my mom walked in.

"Rhae what the hell you done got yourself into baby? You know they could charge you as an adult, which means that you could go away for a long time? Why don't you just tell them the truth? Why are you protecting that no good ass nigga? Baby, if he really gave a fuck about you, he would have never put you in a position where you have to go to jail. This is not the life I wanted for you." mommy replied while wiping tears from her eyes.

"Mommy I know but you don't understand how deep it is. I don't know the type of people Za'Kari is dealing with. And if I tell on Za'Kari, he will kill me!" I whispered to her.

"Oh, now you're scared? You wasn't scared when you were letting him do the shit. You think I'm worried about some punk ass wannabe drug dealer? That nigga does not want me to come out of retirement. Now tell these people what the fuck they want to know and I'm not asking, I'm telling you!" My mom said while getting up and walking out while slamming the door.

Chapter Five

Za'Kari

"Man, what the fuck?"

I rode past Rhae's house this morning after I dropped her off at school so I could pick up my packages and the Feds were running all through her shit. Two detectives were outside talking to one another, and two other detectives were walking out the house carrying the safe I kept all my weed and dope in.

To make matters worse this dumb bitch Rhae texted me, knowing damn well they probably watching her ass. That's what I get for fucking with a young female. They don't fucking listen. I know I told her if some shit ever goes down to not call or text my phone.

I decided to go back to my baby's house because I don't know if they were watching my shit or not. I pulled up to Kazie's house got out and used my key to go in. Yes, you heard me right, Kazie is my baby. My girl's bestie. I mean one drunken night led to two and well you know the rest. I loved Rhae for what she was doing for me, but I wasn't in love with her.

Yeah, she had Kazie beat in the looks department, but Rhae wasn't really my type. She was too clingy and needy. Her pussy was fire though. I was the first to get up in that sweet shit and probably will be the last because all the work they found in her house look like little mama bout to be gone up state for a while.

I would keep money on her books. That was the least I could do. Because a fly nigga like me was not cut out for no jail. Plus, I loved pussy too much. Y'all could call me what you want but I bet I won't do no time. Wanna know why? Because Rhae's scared of me and she knows I'll kill her and her whole fucking family.

I guess you are wondering why I was having the packages delivered to her house. Well it was just me and my brother Zaylen and we were just starting to build our empire. Zaylen was doing his thang on his end and I was doing mine. I didn't trust too many people and I knew I had Rhae's head so gone that she would do whatever I told her to or suffer the consequences. I know you didn't think I was stupid enough to send the shit to my house.

But now this shit happened, it looked like we need to regroup. It looked like Kazie had gone to work, so I decided to call my brother and have him meet me over here.

"Yo what's good, little one?"

"Meet me at Kazie's crib ASAP!"

"Say no more."

While I waited for my brother to come, I decided to fix me something to eat and take a shower. I know Rhae's ass probably sitting up in that bitch scared as hell, but her ass could handle it. She probably gonna get a slap on the wrist. Shit, it's her first offense. I rolled up a fat ass blunt of some of my finest kush I had to offer the D. Before I could even spark up my blunt, my brother was knocking on the door.

"What's the emergency?"

"Man, why the fuck the Feds run up in Rhae's crib today and confiscated all my shit bro. Like what the fuck am I going to do? You know them Jamaicans ain't trying to hear shit but where the money at."

"You have got to be fucking kidding me? Where the fuck is Rhae at?"

"Shit I guess she at the station. I don't know what the fuck I'm gone do."

"Za'Kari, I know you are not about to let little mama take the fall for this shit. That girl only eighteen bruh. She was about to graduate."

"Bro I would rather it be her than me. I mean if they charge me, you know they throwing the book at me. She probably going to get a slap on the wrist since it's her first offense. And to top all that shit off, Kazie's ass is pregnant." I said while lighting my blunt.

"Nigga you on some fuck boy type of shit. Why would you even get her involved? Who the fuck has somebody send fucking drugs in the mail? I mean did you really think that they weren't going to catch on? You gotta be smarter than that. Why didn't you have the packages sent to Kazie's house? She supposed to be your side chick not your main chick. On top of all that, you got her best friend pregnant. Both of y'all on some fuck shit and when that bitch name karma hits y'all asses, she gone hit hard. You always have been selfish." Zaylen replied while shaking his head.

"Bruh, I'm not trying to hear no fucking lecture. Are you going to help a nigga or not?" I asked while inhaling my blunt this whole situation was stressing me the fuck out.

"You sound dumb as hell. How do you know Rhae's not gonna tell them it was yo shit? I know if I was in her shoes, I would be singing like a fucking canary. Now you done ruined another person's life because you only thinking about Za'Kari. So, let me get this straight. You fucking her best friend and now she could possibly get locked up because of your dumbass actions. Let me call my lawyer so they can help that girl. Tell Kazie to help yo dumb ass since she yo rider. I'm out."

Zaylen yelled while walking out and slamming the door.

"Fuck you and her nigga. I'm going to make sure she don't tell." I yelled out the door.

I don't know why this nigga trippin'. He act like he was feeling Rhae or some shit. Let me find out. I wonder what time Kazie's ass get off work. A nigga needed to release some stress. Damn if it ain't one thing it's another.

I decided to take me a nap before Kazie got home because a nigga was higher than a motherfucka and still stressed. I know these Jamaicans was going to be calling for they payment soon. I mean don't get me wrong, I had enough money to keep them off my ass for a little while but not long enough. I needed to find me another plug and quick.

I must have been tired because when I went to sleep it was daylight, and when I woke up, it was dark outside. A nigga was hungry as hell, so I decided to go visit my OG. She always had something to eat. I hopped in the shower and threw on some Jordan basketball shorts and some Jordan slides and a crisp white tee. I sprayed on some of my Dior Sauvage cologne, and put my dreads up into a high ponytail. Looking at my dreads, I made a mental note to make an appointment at Unique Styles to get my shit retwisted. As I was walking out the door, my phone started ringing. I checked to see who was calling and it was Kazie.

"What's up baby? How is work going?" I asked while locking the door.

"You know the police ran up in your bitches house today and she has been trying to get a hold of you." Kazie said while eating her food.

"What she calling me for I don't got shit to do with what's going on in her household." I said while getting in my Audi A7.

"Looks like your precious Rhae is about to go away for a long time I just talked to my Aunt Tish and she said they found a lot of drugs. I guess now would be the best time to tell her she about to be a stepmother." Kazie said while laughing.

I had to look at my phone and make sure I was talking to the right person. Because this bitch was really evil. Why would you even think about telling her that bullshit when her freedom is on the line?

"You worried about the wrong shit little mama. Like I said I ain't got nothing to do with that shit. Now what you need to be worried about is what you going to cook a nigga, and how you gone take this dick when you get home from work. Stay in your lane, Kazie because this ain't got shit to do with you." I said while merging in and out of traffic.

"I mean she is my best friend. Just because I'm fucking you doesn't mean that I don't care about her. I just love your dick more. I am just going to stop answering her calls because I don't feel like making up no lies and hearing her whine. I got fucking problems of my own. Well my lunch is over. I'll see you when I make it home. Don't be out here flirting and shit. I better be the only side chick soon to be main chick!" Kazie said while throwing her food away.

"See what I'm saying? Get off my phone with yo fake ass. You be worried about the wrong shit." I said while hanging up and pulling into my OG driveway.

I used my key to walk in. As usual my OG was in the kitchen whipping up a meal and the aroma was making my stomach growl. Once I made it to the kitchen, I immediately walked to the kitchen sink to wash my hands, because mama don't play that reaching in her pots without washing your hands.

"What's up good lookin'? What you cooking?" I asked while kissing her on the cheek.

"Hey baby. Oh nothing much, just some baked spaghetti with garlic bread and my famous chicken wings. You made it just in time. It's almost finished. So, what's going on with you?" my mother asked while taking the baked spaghetti out of the oven.

"Nothing just chilling. Trying to live my best life while trying to make us rich." I said while grabbing a chicken wing off a plate on the stove.

My OG knew what me and my brother did. Although she didn't agree with it, she still supported us. Back in the day, my OG and pops flooded the Eastside of Detroit with some of the purest cocaine the D had to offer. My mom couldn't take any more of my father's bullshit, from the side chicks and physical abuse, so she gave it all up just so my brother and me could have a stable environment. What's so fucked up is he stayed in the game and was making thousands a week but still let us struggle. He felt like she was disloyal for leaving, so he felt like he didn't have to take care of his family.

It was plenty of nights my mama would be up crying because this nigga didn't come home. Although she knew she would get her ass beat, she always let his ass have it once he walked through that door. Maybe that's why I dogged females because I saw how my daddy used to do my mama. Oh well it's either they rocking with me or their not, either way I'll be good.

"Ok out here living your best life. What's going on between you and my Rhae? How come you didn't bring her with you? I haven't seen her in weeks. Za'Kari you better do right by that girl. Don't be mad when another guy comes and sweeps her off her feet and treats her how she is supposed to be treated." My mother said while fixing me a hefty plate.

"Ma that girl ain't going nowhere literally. Plus she ain't crazy. I'll kill both of them first. Rhae knows I ain't wrapped to tight." I said while eating.

"Boy you sound just like your dumb ass daddy and you gone end up like him too. You gone be left out here lonely, saying she was the one that got away. Watch and see what I tell ya, and don't think you going to move ya ass back in here, because I love being by myself. If I want to wake up and not put on a lick of clothes, I don't have to because I live by myself." My mother said while sitting down at the dining room table.

"Ma too much information." I said while shaking my head.

I chopped it up with my OG for a couple of hours before heading back East to Kazie's house. I wanted to check on my shit first. I needed to check on my fish and check my mail. I still lived in the hood right off 7 mile and Van Dyke. Don't get it twisted, a nigga had enough money to move up out the hood, but why move when you don't have too? I pulled on my block and as usual the same thots were walking up and down the street trying to catch the attention of one of the block boys. These dumb ass niggas were giving them exactly what they were looking for.

When I pulled up to my house, something didn't look right. I sat in my car a few minutes because I did just get done smoking a blunt of that exotic shit. Maybe I was tweaking. Before I could even get all the way out the whip, I heard tires screeching and a car going full speed. Being a hood nigga, those two sounds together meant you better grab yo shit and that's exactly what I did. Next thing I knew, I swear it sounded like World War III right in front of me. Damn all I could think was I got caught slipping by some hoe ass niggas. Instead of shooting back my ass was ducked down in my car praying that none of the bullets hit me.

Then all of a sudden, the gunshots ended and it was silent. I laid there for a minute to make sure they were gone. I knew they weren't coming back to kill me because if they wanted to kill me, they could have about five minutes ago. I jumped out of my car and started feeling all over my body to make sure I wasn't hit or saw blood anywhere. Damn they really tried to take me out. I knew it was them motherfuckin' Jamaican's. I was about to call Winston's ole jerk chicken eating ass. Damn it ain't even been twenty-four hours and this nigga already sending his goons after me. How the fuck did he even know I didn't have the money. What the fuck!

Chapter Six

Rhae

It had been two weeks since I been locked up like some fucking caged animal. They kept trying all kinds of tactics to get me to talk. But shit they don't understand how fucking crazy Za'Kari was. I would rather just sit down and do my time and get the fuck on. I mean I was only eighteen. I still would have time to put my fucked-up life together.

"Inmate you have a visitor."

I wonder who that can be. My mom already came to visit me this week and Kazie's ass hasn't been answering her phone. So, I doubt it's her and I know Za'Kari's ass ain't ever stepping foot in no jail. The CO came in my cell and handcuffed me and guided me to the visitation area.

When I got there, I was surprised to see Zaylen sitting there. *Maybe Za'Kari sent him* I thought to myself. I sat down in front of him and at first, we just sat there staring at each other. I don't know if it was because I hadn't seen him in a minute, or if I never really paid attention to this nigga, but got damn this nigga fine. He stood about six foot four, brown skinned, with hazel eyes and waves for days. He had tattoos all over his body and he had to weigh like two hundred and thirty pounds. He had the most perfect white teeth and a smile that was contagious. His demeanor screamed boss.

Now how the hell did I miss how fine he was, I have no idea. But it's too late now. I've been tainted by a fuck boy. Plus, I wonder if he still talked to Kazie. That's one thing you didn't do and that was go after yo home girl's guy. It was like an unwritten rule. But damn it's hard to turn the attraction off.

"What's good little baby? How you holding up?" Zaylen said while looking at me from head to toe.

Talking about a bitch feeling self-conscious. Here I am looking like one of the chicks off of Orange Is the New Black, and this nigga looking at me like I'm a steak or something.

"Let's see. I missed all my finals so therefore I won't graduate. The food here is horrible. Hell, by the time I get out of here, a bitch gone be skinny because I refuse to eat that shit. Oh, and let's not forget my so called nigga won't answer his phone and hasn't been here to see me not once. Oh, and I want to lay in my own bed. But other than that, just peachy." I said while rolling my eyes.

"Look Rhae, I know it's a fucked-up ass situation, but you're strong. We gone get through this. I got my lawyer coming to see you tomorrow. You're going to need it. Those public defenders can give two fucks about your sexy ass." Zaylen said while looking into my eyes and licking his lips.

"Lawyer Zaylen? I don't have money for a lawyer and I know for damn sure my mom doesn't. She has two other kids she has to take care of." I said while watching him licking his luscious lips.

"I didn't ask you for anything, did I? stop thinking everybody is against you, Ma. I know you used to dealing with fuck boys. But once I show you how a real nigga treats a woman, you not gone have no choice but to expect nothing less. Yeah, my brother did some foul shit because he is selfish. But you had some part in this too because you allowed him to put you in this fucked up situation. Stop thinking everybody your fucking friend." Zaylen said while shaking his head.

"What you mean? You and everybody on the East know I only fuck wit Kazie. No new friends." I replied with much attitude.

"Ma that's exactly who the fuck I'm talking about. While you in here fighting for your freedom, she laid up wit your so called nigga. They been kicking it for a while. It just wasn't my place to tell you." Zaylen replied while folding his hands in front of him on the table.

"Fuck both of them. Karma is a bitch and it's going to fuck both of their asses up. I can't believe they would do me like that after all I did for their asses. This how they repay me?" I said with a tear running down my face. Zaylen reached over and wiped it away.

"Look Ma stop wasting all your energy on people that can give two fucks about you. Now that's the last time I am going to see you drop a tear for either one of those motherfuckas. If don't nobody else got you I do. Plus, if you show any sign of weakness these bitches in here gonna give you hell." Zaylen said.

I nodded my head and wiped my face, but the tears continued to flow. He was right. There was no need to cry over some shit I most definitely couldn't change. Just know once I get out of this hell hole, all those motherfuckas who betrayed me were gon' feel my motherfuckin' wrath.

"Why are you helping me and how do I know I can trust you?" I asked him because at this point everybody suspect.

"Because I'm right here. Think about it, how many visitors have you had since you been locked up Ma? Don't think I'm anything like my punk ass brother because I'm not. If you would have been fucking with me from the jump, you wouldn't have never been involved with this bullshit point blank period. You're too fucking sexy to be locked behind some damn bars like a fucking animal. I already told my brother I ain't fucking with him no more because of this fuck shit he's on. Trust me, that nigga knows how I get down so I ain't worried about shit. Just know I got you, alright?" Zaylen replied with sincerity in his eyes

I wanted to hop over the table and kiss his sexy ass but unfortunately, I couldn't. I just stared at him. I mean he looked and sounded sincere. But who the fuck was I kidding? I thought Za'Kari's ass was a real nigga. Only thing I could do was hope and pray that he was a real nigga. Shit that's all I could do I don't have nothing else to lose.

"Visiting hours are over." The correction officer yelled.

I stood up and he walked around and gave me a hug, and damn did this nigga smelled good. I let him go and this nigga kissed me on the lips. The

CO ain't say shit. I wanted to do more than the little peck, but I didn't want to push my luck.

"Look Ma remember this number. (313) 225-1243, call me tonight. There should be a package waiting on you when you go to the back." Zaylen whispered in my ear.

This nigga just don't know what I wanted to do to his ass whispering in my ear and shit. I smiled and he winked, and I went back to my cell. I'm glad I didn't share a cell with anybody yet, because these bitches were nosey as hell. When I got back to my cell, I had a burner phone under my pillow. Thank God Zaylen had connects on the inside, because those jail phone calls were expensive and I needed to find out if Kazie got a hold of Za'Kari's bitch ass. I looked around to make sure none of the aggravating ass guards were around. Once I made sure the coast was clear I called Kazie's fake ass.

"Hello who the hell is this?" Kazie answered with much attitude.

"It's me you fake bitch. So you been fucking my nigga this whole time knowing all the bullshit he put me through? You were supposed to be my best friend. I would have never done that shit to you. But that's my fault trusting two dis-loyal ass people. Just know when I get out this lil situation, I'm coming for both of y'all trust me. No need to respond back because everything that come out your mouth is fucking lies. You can relay the same message to yo bum ass nigga." I said while hanging up in her face.

I didn't even give her a chance to respond or say some slick shit, because that shit would have made me even madder. I can't believe this bitch betrayed me. I had been there for Kazie when her own bum ass mother wasn't. That shit had to count for something. I guess you fucking live and you learn. I hated Za'Kari's ass too. If that bitch was on fire right now, I would pour more gasoline on his ass for real.

Chapter Seven

It was so fucked up how my brother doing that girl. I mean I don't put it all on him because she allowed him to treat her that way, but at the same time as a grown ass man. It was just some shit you don't do. That little operation he had was dumb as fuck anyway. Who the fuck sends drugs in the mail. His ass needed to be on that show the *World's Dumbest Criminals.*

I know you thinking what type of nigga turns his back on his brother. I'll tell you what kind of nigga who is tired of bailing a nigga out who makes dumb ass decisions. This nigga has been doing this shit since we were kids. Shit I done took a bullet for this nigga and his stupidity.

It was time I started living for Zaylen. Right is right and wrong is wrong. We were supposed to be building an empire, but the way this nigga going, he gon' be behind bars. He was supposed to be in charge of distributing the weed and x pills, and I take care of the rest. Dumb ass nigga couldn't even handle that.

I was not trying to step on this nigga toes by helping Rhae but shit she ain't got nobody else in her corner. Plus, he doesn't deserve her loyalty or her period. I mean technically Rhae was supposed to be mine, he just beat me to it. I saw her first. Hell I even pointed her out. He was supposed to get her attention, not holler at her. Kazie was more of his type. How you gonna holler at both of the females?

Like I told Rhae, my brother knows how I get down. He don't want these problems for real. I mean Rhae is beautiful. She was smart and loyal as fuck. Ain't no way in the hell I would have done her dirty like that. This nigga wanted his cake and eat it too. Well he gone have to let her go because it was a wrap. She not gon' want his ass after this anyway. Once I give her a taste of a real nigga; she will never go back. The heart wants what the heart wants, and I wanted Rhae.

I mean who wouldn't want Rhae? Her mixed features with her caramel skin tone and long, curly hair made could catch the attention of any man. Her body was banging with the perfect set of tits and the perfect sized ass to match. Even with her little stomach, she was still gorgeous. I personally, would have liked for her to have a little more meat. I hated skinny chicks. For one, they think they are better than everyone else. For two, they usually couldn't cook, and three, most couldn't take this dick. Plus, I need something to grab on too and that will keep me warm at night.

It wasn't all about looks though because you could have the baddest bitch, and she could be out here clueless and disloyal. Trust me I know. I done had my share. No real nigga wanted to be out here slanging dope dick to every female they meet. You see Rhae is different. She is intelligent, beautiful and a rider. Look how she rode for my brother. Sometimes we are loyal to the wrong motherfuckas I swear. But she don't have shit to worry about with me because I'm that nigga and I know her worth.

So, trust and believe I was going to do everything in my power to keep her. We hadn't even made shit official and I was staking my claim. I will be her last. Yeah, I know she young, but at twenty-four, I was young too.

I decided to go and check on the work being done to my Hookah Bar. The grand opening was coming up soon and I wanted to make sure everything was being done right. I was far from a dumb nigga. I always told myself whenever I made just enough money to invest, I would. I could never understand why niggas be in the game for so long. The whole purpose of getting in the game is to give you a head start on securing the bag for life legally.

When I pulled up, my manager Will was talking to the construction workers. Will and I have been rocking since we were kids, pinching the little girls in the neighborhood asses and running. I trusted this nigga with my life and vice versa. The only difference between Will and me is he is definitely the definition of a man whore. This fool changed women like he changes his draws. The

Hookah Bar was coming along. I just wish Rhae was here to be on my arm at the grand opening. It was small shit to a giant. I am going to have her out of there in no time. I walked up to Will just as he was finishing up talking to the construction worker.

"Tell me something good bro." I said while slapping hands with him and giving him a manly hug.

"Nah bruh, I need to be asking you that question because Shauntae just left from here looking for you, and the only time she comes around is if your ass did something to get in trouble with the law." Will said while walking beside me going into the building.

"Man watch your mouth. You know damn well I haven't been in any trouble because yo ass would have been the one coming down to the 6th precinct to bail my ass out. I don't know why she came by here when she could have just called me." I said while shaking my head.

"Don't try to sit there and act like you got amnesia nigga. You know why Shauntae came by here. She wants her baby daddy back. I never understood how you fucked with her bougie ass. It was like y'all was from two different worlds. Now that she is an attorney, the bougieness has gotten worse. She walks around this motherfucka like she better than everybody, when she got more skeletons in her closet than me and you put together." Will said while walking into his office.

"You know I know and quit calling me her baby daddy. You know damn well we don't have any kids together. I don't care what she wants back. She knows I ain't going down that road. I just need her to do me this one solid so I can help baby girl out in this situation." I said while sitting down.

"Wait, time out. Flag on the play. Who is your baby girl because last chick I remember you messing around with was Kazie's thot ass and y'all was just fucking occasionally." Will said while pouring himself a shot of Hennessy.

"Man, hell nah. I wouldn't help her if she begged me to. She's useless. Her ass better call Za'Kari's ass. I'm talking about Rhae. Za'Kari done fucked around and got her house raided because he had the Jamaicans sending his work through the mail. Now he's letting her take the fall for it. He on some fuck boy shit. She doesn't deserve none of that at all, so I'm having Shauntae help her. Hell I pay her ass enough." I said while pouring myself a drink.

"Damn that's fucked up, but that's what's up. I am glad you are helping her. Real men do real things. Rhae's fine as hell with her thick ass. I would have been taken her off of Za'Kari's hands. She was just too young. You know I like them cougars." Will said while laughing

"Watch yo mouth. That's all me. You gone get enough fucking around with them old ass women. Man let me do a walk through and get out of here and go holla at Shauntae's ass. I'm going to holla at you later." I said while slapping hands with him and leaving out his office.

Walking around my establishment made me feel like a proud father. I worked so hard to get where I am right now. I did it all without having to kill anybody or going to jail. I always made my moves strategically. I wasn't no typical nickel and dime hustler. I moved weight. I had been doing this shit since I was sixteen and now I'm twenty-four. My brother don't even know how deep in this shit I was. Nobody knows that I was the fucking plug. I was very powerful in these streets. That was why I walked around like I had an S on my chest. I ain't got no worries. The only thing I had to do was make one phone call and I could have you and your whole family taken out. I was going to hand this shit over to my brother, but as you could see, this nigga was dumb. He would fuck around and take my whole operation under.

After walking through the bar and checking everything out, I decided to head over to Shauntae's office to make sure she was doing what I fucking paid her to do. There was no reason for her to be just popping up without calling. I don't belong to her, and even if I did, I'm a grown ass man. Will left before me so I made sure to lock up everything, Just as I was locking up, I heard a car door slam. I turned around and noticed it was Za'Kari. I shook my head because I knew this nigga was about to be on some straight bullshit and how did he know where I was anyway?

"What's up Za'Kari? I was just about to shoot a move so make it quick." I said while walking towards my truck.

"Damn whatever it is, it can wait. I really need your help right now. It's life or death." Za'Kari said while inhaling the smoke from his blunt.

"Nah what I gotta do can't wait, so like I said make it quick. What's up?" I said while stopping and looking him dead in his eyes.

"Man, whatever. Look I need to borrow like fifty bands, so I can pay the Jamaicans off. Can you believe these crazy motherfuckas did a drive by and almost took your only blood brother out?" Za'Kari said while shaking his head.

See what I am saying? This fool was always writing a check that his ass couldn't cash. I never was fronted shit because I don't like having to owe the next nigga. That's where these so-called dope boys went wrong. Be your own fucking boss. I could call Winston and have this shit with my brother settled, but if I continued to bail him out, then he would never learn his lesson. So I wasn't getting in his shit.

"Most people ask to borrow a few hundred or even a few thousand, and then there is you. The nigga who don't give a fuck about nobody but himself. Man, hell nah I'm not loaning you shit. Nobody has fifty bands to just loan out. Not even to Jesus himself. Let's just call this your karma for how you're doing Rhae. You better get out here and get it how you live." I said while walking around him and going towards my truck.

"So, you just gonna let this nigga and his goons take me out over a punk ass fifty thousand dollars that you do have? As far as Rhae goes, that's my bitch and I'll handle that. Don't worry about her." Za'Kari said while grabbing my arm to stop me.

"Bruh let my arm go and no I'm not loaning you shit. You always getting yourself in some shit you can't get out of. I told you before you even got involved with that nigga Winston make sure you were on yo shit. You a grown ass man. Start acting like one." I said while unlocking my truck and snatching my arm out of his hand and getting in my truck and pulling off on his dumb ass.

I swear to God that nigga made my blood hurt for real. I can't believe this nigga really had the nerve to even come and ask me for $50,000 dollars, when he know damn well he not going to pay me back. He never did. That's Za'Kari's problem he thinks the world owe him something when don't nobody owe his ass shit. I am not about to keep bailing a grown ass man out, brother or not. I am not about to continue to dwell on what the next nigga got going. I got other shit I had to worry about like why Shauntae's ass kept looking for me.

I made my way onto the lodge freeway heading downtown Detroit. I was glad it was the earlier part of the day because traffic would have been a motherfucka during rush hour. I hoped Shauntae was not on no bullshit because I was not fucking with her like how she wanted me too. Due to it not being any traffic on the lodge, I made it to Shauntae's office in no time. I parked and made my way into the building. When I made it inside, there was this fine ass chick sitting at the receptionist desk. If I wasn't already pursuing little mama Rhae, I promise she would have been my next choice. I flashed her my signature smile with all thirty-two of my pearly whites.

"Um excuse me sweetheart. Could you please let Shauntae know that there is a Zaylen here to see her?" I said while still smiling.

"My name is not sweetheart, it's Maria. Do you have an appointment Mr. Zaylen?" Maria said while rolling her hazel brown eyes.

Forget everything I just said about this ratchet bitch. Her attitude was so ugly. I mean damn, all I did was call her sweetheart, which I thought was a sweet gesture. I bet if I walked in here yelling and being hood, her whole attitude would be totally different. I guess she never heard of the saying never judge a book by its cover.

"No, I don't have an appointment, but I guarantee that if you pick up that thing in front of you called a phone, you would see that she is expecting me.' I said while pointing to the phone on her desk.

"Well if you don't have an appointment, then I would need to schedule an appointment for you to see Ms. Woods, because she gave me strict orders not to bother her unless the client has an appointment. Now what would be a good day for you to come back? It does look like she has an opening tomorrow morning around nine." The receptionist said while looking at her computer screen.

Why must everybody get on my damn nerves today? I don't even know why I tried to act civilized toward people. I am not about to sit here and go back and forth with this chick about no damn appointment, when all she had to do is pick up the damn phone and let Shauntae know I am here. I just walked right passed her ass and started making my way towards Shauntae's office. As I walked toward the door, I could hear her screaming that I couldn't go back there, but I wasn't paying her ass no attention. I tried to be nice now I had to do shit my way. Once I made it to her office, I didn't even bother knocking. I just walked right in and Shauntae was looking down at some papers on her desk.

"I told you sir you can't come back here, and you just walked right passed me like I didn't say anything. Now please leave before I call the police." The receptionist said to me out of breath.

"And I told your incompetent ass that Ms. Woods was expecting me and that I don't have to have a fucking appointment. Now Shauntae tell your little employee that we are good." I said while sitting in a chair in front of Shauntae's desk.

"Ms. Woods, I apologize I tried to schedule him an appointment for tomorrow, but he was determined to see you now." The receptionist said while mugging me.

I wanted to laugh at her ass trying to sound all professional, when her ass was just rude a few minutes ago. Shauntae was looking back and forth like we were crazy, but I didn't care because I was just here to make sure she was doing everything she could to get my baby girl off.

"That's okay, Maria. He is fine. Can you close the door behind you and hold all my calls for the rest of the afternoon?" Shauntae said while getting out of her seat.

"Not a problem Ms. Woods like I stated before I apologize." Maria said while walking out the door and closing it.

"I see you are the same Zaylen. Everything has to be done on your terms. What brings you to my neck of the woods? I came by your Hookah Bar earlier to talk to you about Za'Kari's girlfriends' case, but as usual, you were nowhere to be found. You probably were laying up with one of your thots." Shauntae said while rolling her eyes.

Here comes the bullshit. She already got me ready to run up out of here. I don't know how many times I had to tell a motherfucka that I don't want nothing to do with them.

"Man go head on with that bullshit you on. I am a grown ass man and if I want to be laid up with fifty bitches, it ain't your concern. You didn't even have to go to the Hookah Bar. You could have just called me and told me what the fuck was going on. Don't act like you don't know my number Shauntae. Now that's out the way, what do you want?" I said while looking at her in her eyes.

"Zaylen don't you think you have been mad at me long enough? Damn. How long are you going to make me suffer? I learned from my mistakes. I am ready for us to get back to us." Shauntae said while coming and sitting in my lap. This girl thought sex could get her out of anything. I ain't gone lie to y'all though, the girl's sex game was official, and my dick was standing at attention. But if I was to bend her over right now and fuck the shit out of her, she would think that meant that we were back together. So, to avoid all the drama I just had to have willpower and get to the real reason why I was here.

"Shauntae get the fuck off me and tell me what the fuck is going on with Rhae's case." I said while pushing her out of my lap.

"Damn Zaylen, you are real worried about this chick for her to be Za'Kari's girlfriend. Let me find out you're checking for this bitch, or she one of your side chicks. The bitch would never see the light of day if I had something to do with it. I was coming to see you to let you know the best option for her is to take a plea deal because she will not tell them anything and basically, all evidence points towards her. I know if I was her ass, I would tell on everybody." Shauntae advised.

"Damn how long are we talking? I mean it is her first offense and she has never been in trouble at all." I asked with a concerned look on my face.

"Five to ten years with a possibility of parole in three. I swear you act like she's more than just Za'Kari's girlfriend. Where is Za'Kari at anyway? Shouldn't I be talking to him and not you?" Shauntae asked with a raised eyebrow.

"That offer is not good enough. I am going to need you to work your little magic and get a better fucking deal than that. That girl ain't have shit to do with none of that shit. I pay your ass very well so instead of you worrying about what the fuck I got going on, you need to be figuring this shit out like yesterday!" I said while standing up and walking towards the door.

I was pissed. It was so fucked up that my brother was doing Rhae like that. This girl basically was about to serve time for a nigga that could give two fucks about her. I mean what type of nigga would let they woman go to jail for anything? I wish I had a way to turn back the hands of time, because I swear to God Rhae's life would be totally different. I would have talked to her first and she would have never talked to Za'kari's bitch ass. I must have been in deep thought because I didn't hear Shauntae talking to me and I stopped walking.

"HELLO!" Shauntae yelled.

"What? Damn, I got shit to do and so do you." I said while turning around to face her thirsty ass again.

"I said I would see what I can do but there is not much I can do." Shauntae said while walking up to me.

"You better do something. You better put those pretty lips around a judge's dick or something. Now get her a better fucking deal or it's not going to be a good outcome for you, and you know how I operate!" I said while kissing her on the cheek and walking out.

Chapter Eight

Za'Kari

It had been two months since Rhae had been locked up. I hadn't talked to her or went to go see her. I didn't want to chance it because I know the feds watched her every move. Do I feel a little bad? Yes, but not really. Better her than me. I mean this only her first offense she would survive.

I turned over and this bitch Kazie was lying next to me. What the fuck was I thinking fucking with this bitch? At first it was all good. She was doing everything for a nigga. She was cooking, cleaning, fucking, and giving me some fiyah ass head on the regular. Now all the bitch did was spend my money like she Queen Sheba or some motherfuckin' body.

I decided I would go visit Rhae today. I mean it had been two months since she saw me, and she just stop calling me out of the blue. I know she got me on her visiting list because she loved me, and who else would visit her besides her mom? I made sure I was her everything. Call me selfish I don't give a fuck.

I decided to get up early and go visit. Maybe I could brighten up her day. I know she gotta be in there depressed. I hopped in the shower and handled my hygiene. I brushed my teeth and put my dreads up in a messy bun. I decided to put on some Jordan joggers with a crisp white T and some black and white Jordan 12s. I put my diamond studs in my ear with my Jesus piece.

"Bae where you going?" Kazie asked while stretching.

Even this bitches voice was irritating as hell.

"I'm grown as hell and last time I checked, my mama's name was Barbara Jean not Kazie. I'm going out by myself," I said while grabbing my car keys off the dresser.

"Well, damn. Who pissed in your Cheerios this morning? Well I guess I'll take my ass back to sleep. Can you leave me some money? I need a fill in and my hair done. Tonight, is Zaylen's grand opening to his Hookah Bar." Kazie said while laying back down.

"I'm not leaving you shit and you're not going. How the fuck you gone go to my brother's shit without me? I told you we not fucking with each other like that. Let me find out you checking for that nigga." I said while walking out of the room.

"Za'Kari ain't nobody checking for shit and how you gone tell me I can't go? Everybody gone be there. He's been advertising all over the radio. What happened between y'all anyway?" Kazie asked while following me to the front door.

You see why I say she's fucking irritating? The bitch was nosey as hell, and her ass acted like she couldn't sit the fuck down. She always got to talk back like she was the man in this fucked up ass relationship.

How the hell did I end up here in a relationship with this bitch anyway? Let me get the fuck on before I smack this bitch for real.

"You heard what the fuck I said. You not fucking going. Try to go if you want to and I'm gone come up in that motherfucka and drag yo ass out. Now try me if you want to." I said while walking out the door and slamming it.

"Za'Kari yo ass ain't my daddy, but I don't feel like arguing with yo dumb ass, so I'll just sit in the house bored as hell. You get on my fucking nerves." Kazie said while opening the door and slamming it back.

I was about to go back in the house and choke this bitch. Her ass was lucky I had somewhere to be. I just shook my head and pulled out the driveway. Visiting hours were about to start and I didn't want to miss seeing Rhae.

I arrived at the jail thirty minutes later. I hated all the shit you got to go through just to see a loved one behind bars. After being checked in, they took us to the back to the visiting area. I didn't know why I was nervous seeing Rhae. I know she would be happy to see me.

Once the inmates started coming in, I kept watching the door and Rhae finally walked in. She looked like she lost some weight and was looking damn good. I mean she didn't even look like she was stressing. She sat down in front of me and was just mugging me.

"Well hello to you, bae." I said while smiling.

"What the fuck do you want Za'Kari? Why are you even here?" Rhae asked while slamming her hand on the table.

"Because you still my girl and I'm supposed to be here. What you mean? Look, bae I'm sorry about how shit went down. But you my rider, right? We gon' get through this shit. Who you think been keeping money on your books? I know you pissed bae, but I had to stay away. You know that. You know I love you right?" I said while touching her hand.

She started laughing hard as hell like I was a fucking comedian or some shit.

"My man? Nigga you stopped being my man the second I heard them doors lock. You think this shit a game? Nigga we talking about my motherfuckin' life. I'm about to lose years of my life that I can't get fucking back because of my so-called man. What's so fucked up is I was once your rider and loved everything about yo bum ass. I risked everything for yo bitch ass and what do you do? You pay me back by fucking my best friend and leaving me to rot up in this motherfucka. I'm not even mad though since I ain't no snitching ass bitch. I'm gone take whatever the judge gives me and I'm gone rock it out like I'm supposed to. You ain't gotta say shit to me ever. You a fuck boy and I have no room in my life for those." Rhae said while sitting back in her seat.

"Bae." I said while trying to hold her hand once again.

"My name is Rhae. That's what you need to address me by. You never loved me. You don't love nobody but your damn self. Oh yeah and tell yo bitch Kazie that I'm coming for that ass. I don't know when. Just know when I'm free, it's on. I can't stand an ungrateful, disloyal motherfucka. Y'all just released a beast and I coming to fuck up some shit. Don't believe me just watch! CO, I'm ready." Rhae said while standing up.

I watched her walk out. Bae didn't even say bye or nothing damn. I liked the new Rhae. But how the hell did she know about me and Kazie? Damn. I do love her. I just got some fucked up ways. I blamed that shit on my punk ass daddy watching the way he treated my OG and side bitches had me thinking it was the right thing to do. I mean what young man doesn't look up to their father? Now that way of thinking may have made me lose the love of my life. Naw she better had thought twice if she thinks I'm going to let her leave me.

I hope she doesn't think this shit is over because it wasn't. She must have forgot who the fuck I was. I ain't gonna lie though, she did just leave a nigga speechless. It kind of hurt to know she thought of me as a fuck nigga though. There was a time when a nigga did no wrong.

All a nigga had to do was say a couple of I love you's and I was sorry and I was back in her good graces, but I guess that was the old Rhae, because the new Rhae wasn't having that shit. That's ok. I was going to give her a little time to get over this bullshit we were going through.

I left the jail all in my feelings because I wasn't the type of guy to be rejected by no female, let alone Rhae. I had other shit I needed to be worrying about, like how the hell I was going to come up with this $50,000 to pay this hoe ass nigga Winston. The only other person besides my punk ass brother that I know got money like that was my sperm donor. That's the least he could do since he ain't did shit else. I hated even asking this nigga for anything, but a niggas life was on the line and I was desperate.

It didn't take me long to get to pops house because his house wasn't too far from Zaylen's Hookah bar on the Eastside of Detroit. When I pulled into the driveway, his two guards were guarding the door like this nigga was President

Obama or some shit. I just shook my head because this fool did the most. The more I thought about it, the more I realized how fucked up my father was, and the more I thought about it, I was the exact same way.

Maybe the way I was treating Rhae was wrong. Maybe I should go downtown and confess that the drugs were mine and that she had nothing to do with it. Man, hell nah. Let me get out my fucking feelings. If I did that, they gone throw the book at my ass, and a nigga like me definitely didn't belong behind nobody's bars.

If she do me this one solid, I'm definitely putting a ring on her finger you don't find loyal bitches like that anymore. Most of the females these days only care about what you can do for them. To be honest Rhae never really asked me for shit but the latest Jordan's or the newest bath and body works, and to keep her hair done. She not really into all those name brand clothes that these thots be busting it wide open with the local dope boys for.

Damn I got to get my baby out this shit I thought to myself. I got out the car and walked up to the house.

"What's up Za'Kari? What brings you around these parts?" Joc the head of security asked.

"Shit, just need to holla at the old man for a second." I said while entering my code to get in the house.

When I walked in, the aroma of some good ass Kush hit my nose. I just followed the smell to where my pops was, which was in the man cave.

"What's up old man?" I asked while sitting on the sofa across from him.

"What do you want Za'Kari? The only reason your ass come to visit is when you need some money that I'm not going to give you." Big Al replied while inhaling his Kush.

"Damn tell me how you really feel. How you know I didn't come over here just to check up on you?" I asked while snatching the blunt out of his hand.

"First of all boy, you better act like you got some damn sense and respect me before I forget you came from my fucking nut sack. Don't you ever snatch shit from my hands. Now how I know you didn't just come over here to check up on me is because you're selfish and don't care about nobody but yourself. You think the world owes you something, but I'm here to tell you don't nobody owe you shit. You walk around all day looking for a handout. That's why I would never pass my business over to you. Now I'm only going to ask you one time and one time only. What the fuck do you want?" Big Al asked while snatching the blunt back and inhaling it.

Damn this some crazy shit. What happened to the meaning of family? When a family member was in trouble, I thought family was supposed to help each other out. The way he was carrying on, I didn't even want to ask this nigga for shit. I mean the least this nigga could do was loan me the money, since he left my mama to raise me and my brother with absolutely no help. Just thinking about the shit made me want to shoot this fool right between his fucking eyes. So instead of doing some fuck shit that I would regret, I just got up and left. Fuck him and my brother. I would figure this shit out on my own.

Chapter Nine

Zaylen

Today was going to be a good day. My first Hookah Bar grand opening was tonight. Everybody that's somebody in Detroit was going to be there. It was about to be so lit. The only thing that's missing was Rhae by my side, shutting shit down. It was cool because this would definitely not be my last grand opening.

Before I got too busy, I decided to go see lil mama. I wanted to see her today because her trial started tomorrow, and I want her to be relaxed. I told her I had her and that's exactly what I was going to do; be right there by her side.

I had a little connect on the inside who was going to give us about thirty minutes to ourselves. Shit I needed to feel little mama something serious. Her ass was just too damn sexy. Plus, a nigga was tired of using lotion. I needed to get this nut off for real.

I got to the jail and checked in. I seen my boy waiting for me to take me to the little spot. He blessed me so I blessed him with a stack. I truly believed in a favor for a favor.

"You know yo brother was here earlier visiting little mama today."

"Oh yeah and how did that shit play out?"

"Man, when I say little mama gave him the business. She got up and left that nigga sitting there looking dumb as hell. I wanted to tell that nigga to fix his face, but you know how hot headed that nigga is," The CO said while laughing.

We both started laughing. I could only imagine what little mama said. These last few months she had changed and for the better. I was really digging little mama and we are becoming closer and closer. Over the past few months I was able to get to know Rhaelyn. True enough, we already knew each other from the hood, and of course from her being around us due to her being in a relationship with my brother, but I got to know her dreams, fears, and life goals. You could ask me anything about her from what she like to do, on down to her bra and shoe size. It was like my day wouldn't go right unless I heard her voice, and although she was in jail, I would still get mad if she didn't answer. I guess you could say I had it bad.

Little mama walked into the room with her face all frowned up, but when she saw it was me, she started smiling extra hard. I don't know about you, but when somebody smiled and it was because of you, it did something to you.

"What's up beautiful? How are you today?"

"Hi Zaylen. I'm good. I was just about to braid my hair for tomorrow. What are you doing here? Shouldn't you be getting ready for tonight?"

"I wanted to see my good luck charm first."

She was blushing hard as hell, and then she just burst out crying.

"Little mama what's wrong? You know I hate seeing you cry. Now talk to me."

"It's just that I don't know what the hell is going to happen tomorrow. I could go away for five to ten years, and because of some shit somebody else did. That's just so fucked up in so many ways."

"Beautiful didn't I say I got you? You are not about to do no five to ten years, trust me. All I need you to do is go in there looking like a boss wit yo game face on and let my lawyer handle the rest, ok?"

She nodded her head. She looked so damn sexy. I couldn't resist. I leaned over and kissed her lips. How the hell they were so soft, I don't know but got damn. I started off with a few pecks then I added some tongue action. I pulled away and looked into her eyes.

Damn she was sexy as hell. It as like I was addicted to her lips. I couldn't stop kissing her. She started moaning and pulling on my shirt. Her moans alone were enough to make me nut prematurely. Fuck this shit. I lifted my shirt and dropped my pants. I hurried up and undressed little mama. When my hands made it to her wet box, it was hot and ready.

We didn't have much time. I hated to do little mama like this, but a nigga was backed up. I turned her around and bent her over on the table. I slid my dick into her tight wet pussy. I mean the shit was so wet, her juices were running down my leg.

"Damn baby. This shit so motherfuckin' tight and wet. You know this shit mine right?"

"Oh damn bae. It's so big. Give it to me. Shit you hitting my spot. I'm about to cum."

"Cum all over this motherfucka. Cum on yo dick bae."

On demand she came all over this motherfucka. I swear the shit was so good, I wanted to scream like a bitch. Now I was far from a minute man, but when the pussy was this good, you couldn't help but to be.

We finished just in time because my mans was knocking on the door to tell us our time was about up. We cleaned up the best we could and got dressed. I kissed her again.

"You know you mine, right?"

"Let's enjoy the moment, Zaylen. You know I'm about to be locked up for a while and I don't want to have to be in here wondering if you faithful or not. Let's just leave it as it is as friends. That would be selfish of me to expect anything more from you. You have done more than enough already."

I grabbed her face and looked into those beautiful gray eyes. I just stared at her for a minute, because for the life of me, I couldn't understand how anyone could betray this beautiful woman in front of me. But you know how this shit goes. Another man's trash is another man's treasure.

"Now you listen to me Ma, and this is the last time I am going to tell you this shit. I am not a fuck nigga. I don't see nobody else but you, so it doesn't matter how long you get, I'm going to be the one waiting on you when you walk out those gates. So don't tell me what you shouldn't expect because you should expect me to be faithful because I am. Baby, if a motherfucka can't support you at your worst they definitely shouldn't be around you when you are at your best. Now give me a kiss and get dressed."

After getting our clothes back on, I knocked on the door.

"Call me later Ma. I'll see you tomorrow at court."

She nodded her head and walked out. Man, Shauntae better not let her do more than a year because it was getting harder and harder to see her walk away. Speaking of the devil, as I was walking out, Shauntae was walking in. I ain't going to lie, Shauntae was looking good as hell with her thick ass. Shauntae was what you call slim thick. She stood about five foot six, with Hershey chocolate skin with big round gray eyes. She had the pinkest lips that if you didn't know her, you would have thought she was wearing lipstick. She always wore her hair in its natural state. She could wear it in her curly state or a blowout. Either one looked good on her. Like right now, she was wearing it straight with the part down the middle, making me have a flashback of how I used to be hitting it from the back and pulling on that shit. I ain't going to lie, Shauntae was definitely a niggas weakness, but she was toxic and could fuck up your whole life and have you blaming yourself.

"Hey Zaylen. I was going to come and see you once I left here visiting your brother's girlfriend." Shauntae said while walking up on me.

Damn she even had on my favorite scent that country apple from Bath and Body Works. She knew what she is doing. But I knew what really was underneath all that beauty and it was pure evil. It took me a long time to get her out of my system and I am not going down that road again.

"Oh yeah and why were you coming to see me? As long as you're doing your job, we have nothing to talk about. I'm not the one in jail. Stop just popping up on me. We are not in a relationship and I don't know how many times I have to tell you this." I said while backing up and putting some space between us.

"You're still mad at me baby? You should be over that shit by now. We were young and dumb back then, and you did some fucked up shit to me too. You know we were in no position to take care of a child. I did the right thing for both of us. Now look at us. I'm a lawyer and you are an established businessman. You think we could have accomplished that with a kid?" Shauntae asked while folding her arms.

"Man, if you don't get the fuck on with that bullshit. You made that choice for your own selfish reasons. You don't know what the fuck I was in the position to do because you never fucking asked." I said while pointing my finger in her beautiful face.

"Zaylen, why are we sitting here arguing about some shit that happened a long time ago? You know you still love and want me just like I love and want you. So, stop fighting what's meant to be." Shauntae said while trying to kiss me.

"No, I don't want you. Do I still have love for you? Yes and I always will. But you and I will never be. Plus, I got a woman, and I don't think she would like it too much if she saw you trying to put your lips on me." I said while curving her ass.

"Quit lying, nigga. You know I got eyes everywhere and we both know you don't have a woman. Well if you do have a woman, I am not worried about her ass because you're mine, so she better get used to this cute ass face." Shauntae said while walking away.

Only thing I could do is just shake my head because I know this heifer is about to run my damn blood pressure up. There was no way in hell I was going to tell her that Rhae was my woman, because she would make sure that they threw my baby in jail and threw the key away. Anything to keep her away from me. I never understood why people, especially women, tried to force people to be with them. If someone tells you, they don't want you they don't want you. I hope Rhae was strong enough to deal with all the bullshit that was about to come our way, because it was definitely going to be a storm coming our way. I could feel it. Nobody is going to want to see us together.

Chapter Ten

After leaving the jail, I decided to go and see my old lady. I knew she is going to curse my ass out because I hadn't been there to see her. I pulled up and I noticed that Za'Kari's truck was outside. I let out a long sigh because I just left my baby, and I was in a good mood. I don't feel like dealing with the bullshit.

I hopped out of my Audi and went into the house using my key. As soon as I opened the door, the aroma of food cooking hit my nose. My stomach started growling instantly.

"Ma where you at?" I yelled while walking through the house looking for her.

"Boy if you don't quit yelling in my damn house, I know something. We are in the kitchen." My mom yelled.

When I got in the kitchen, ma dukes and Za'Kari were sitting at the table eating a feast for a king. I mean she had fried chicken, mac and cheese, cabbage, yams, potato salad, and cornbread. The only thing I was thinking about was how I was about to smash this good food ma dukes had cooked. I washed my hands, grabbed me a plate and sat down across from Za'Kari. You could cut the tension in the room with a knife. I mean no one was talking and the only thing you heard was forks hitting plates.

"What's going on between you two? Why y'all sitting here like some strangers and not brothers?" ma dukes asked while wiping her mouth with a napkin.

"Ma dukes, we straight. I'm just hungry as hell. Plus I got things to do with my Hookah bar opening tonight." I replied while taking a bite of my fried chicken.

"Yeah we good. I just got a lot on my mind. I went to the jail to see my baby and she cursed my ass out. She will get over it though. I'm just going to give her a little space." Za'Kari answered while mugging me.

"Za'Kari you can't be serious son. Did you forget you're the reason why that poor girl is in jail in the first place? On top of that, yo ass messing with her so called best friend. Ain't no coming back from that. The best thing you can do for that girl is leave her alone." Ma dukes replied while getting up from the table.

"Nah, ma. I can't do that. I just realized she was the realest on my team. My actions might not show it, but I love that girl. Matter of fact when I leave here, I'm going to tell Kazie's ass that it's over." Za'Kari replied.

I put my fork down hard as hell and ma dukes stopped talking and looked at me like I lost my mind. But I just lost my fucking appetite. This nigga got life so fucked up if he thought he was coming for my baby. Fuck it. I was just going to tell his ass now that she was mine. Where had his ass been for the last two months? He loved her so much, but he has yet to see what has been going on with her case and today was the first time he even attempted to go visit her? This nigga was a clown.

How do you leave your girl in her time of need? Especially when you're the reason why she is in the fucked-up situation she is in now? You didn't hurt the people you love. You were supposed to protect them and keep them out of harm's way.

Well he don't have to worry about it because I was the one that had been there for Rhae since she had been behind that jail cell. I was the one my baby called when she felt like giving up and spazzing the fuck out. I was the one that went and visited her twice a week without hesitation. I was the one who paid for her attorney. If it was up to him, he would have let her go with a court appointed attorney and we all know they don't give a fuck about what's wrong or right. Shit I done invested my time, feelings, and emotions into Rhae and I would be damned if I just let her go like that.

"Bruh ain't no you and Rhae no more. She's good." I said while looking Za'Kari in his eyes.

"Nigga what the fuck you mean she's good? How the fuck you know she's good? Oh, let me guess you and Rhae together now? I was wondering how the fuck she knew about Kazie. All along it was yo hating ass. My own flesh and blood. How you going to go against yo blood nigga? What type of fuck shit you on?" Za'Kari said while mugging me.

"Nigga ain't nobody got to hate on yo bum ass. She figured out that you were a fuck boy on her own. I didn't have to tell her shit. Now as far as us being together. Yeah, she's mine and I ain't giving her up. You see, I realized my baby's potential. I know what type of woman she is. You know what they say once they get introduced to a real nigga, they hate lames. Now I'm only going to tell you this once. Leave Rhae the fuck alone." I said while standing up.

He started laughing and he got up. I was mugging this nigga hard as hell because I knew he was a hot head and ain't no telling what this nigga was going to do. I didn't want to tear ma dukes house up, but if this nigga tried it, we was about to tear this motherfucka up today. I would just have to pay for the shit later.

Just as I expected, he started walking away but turned around and tried to rush me. I stood up and rocked his ass and he fell and broke ma dukes glass table. He was laying there for a minute, but I knew this shit wasn't over. He got up and rocked my ass back. We were going blow for blow then we heard a gunshot of course we stopped.

"You two motherfuckas done lost your everlasting minds. If you think y'all about to tear my house up, you got me fucked up. Clean this shit up and get the fuck out. Oh and leave my money for the damages on the counter. Don't come back until you both can act like you got some got damn sense." Ma dukes said with her gun in her hand.

She walked away mugging our asses. We didn't say shit because ma dukes was crazy as hell. She would shoot our asses with no hesitation. We both cleaned up the mess. I grabbed my keys so I could leave. I reached in my pocket and pulled out five stacks and left it on the counter.

"You know this shit ain't over, right? You think I'm going to let you take my girl? You got life fucked up. She's just using you to get back at me. See, I was her first everything. She knows daddy loves her." Za'Kari said yelling.

I laugh at this dumb ass nigga, because either he was in denial or he was just dumb as hell.

"You may have been her first nigga, but I'm definitely her last. I would be tripping too bro because the pussy is definitely A1. Trust me, I know. But the difference between me and you is I'm not going to fuck up. That's wifey. We will be sure to send you an invite to the baby shower and wedding. But I'm not about to stand up here and argue with you. You heard what the fuck I said. Stay away from Rhae" I said while walking out the door.

I got in my car and pulled off. I knew this shit wasn't over with Za'Kari because he hated losing. He better had accepted this loss because like I said earlier, she was mine and I didn't plan on letting her go. Not for him not for any fucking body.

Chapter Eleven

Rhae

My graduation was three months ago and instead of me walking across that stage to get my diploma and making my mama proud, I was about to go in this courtroom and stand before a judge who could lock me away for a long time. One bad decision could lead to a lifetime of pain. I wish I would have never been on Belle Isle that day. I wish I would have never talked to Za'Kari's ass. I wish I would have listened to my Mama.

Too late now. The only thing I could do was pray that this judge was not a bitch and cut me some slack seeing that I had never been in trouble before. I needed to talk to my baby because he was the only one that could calm my nerves. I looked out to make sure the coast was clear. It was so I pulled my burner out and called him.

Zaylen was my peace. Over the last few months, he has showed me how a Queen was supposed to be treated by her King. When I was having a bad day, he knew exactly what to say. He had accepted my flaws and all. I mean this man had paid all my attorney fees, knowing damn well my mother and I had no money whatsoever to pay him back. I used to think that the falling in love quick was just for the movies or in the urban fiction books, but when you have a man that sees that you're broken, and he still stays; yeah he was definitely a keeper.

If someone were to ask me right now if I still loved Za'Kari, the answer would be yes. You just couldn't turn this love shit off and on. Is Za'Kari toxic? Yes. Do I want him back? Hell nah. I would never take Za'Kari back. He had done too much to me. I could forgive, but I couldn't forget what he did to me. He was not going to be able to give me the years of my life that I wasted back, and even if he could, my feelings would remain the same. I did way too much for him, and for him to just shit on me like that fuckin' hurt. When a motherfucka hurt you that deep, it started to fuck with your mental. It had me second guessing myself making me think it was my fault the reason why he treated me the way he did. Then along comes Zaylen. My knight and shining armor. He made me realize my worth and that I didn't have to take the bullshit. I knew my worth. I know two wrongs didn't make it right and I was wrong for being with Zaylen. At this point, I really don't care what people thought about our relationship as long as I was happy, that was all that matters.

"Good Morning beautiful. How are you doing this morning?" Zaylen said in his sleepy voice.

"Hey baby. Did I wake you?" I asked

"No, I was woke, but even if I wasn't, you know I would have answered. What are you doing?" Zaylen asked while sitting up in bed.

"Nothing just got out the shower about to get dressed for court. Thank you for the outfit. I really just wanted to hear your voice to calm my nerves. I don't think I ever prayed so hard in my life." I replied, trying not to cry.

"Baby stop worrying. We got this. All I need you to do is come in that courtroom looking beautiful, and yo man gone be sitting right behind you. Now go get dressed, Ma and I'll see you in a minute. I love you." Zaylen said smiling.

"You what Zaylen?" I asked.

"You heard me Ma. I said I love you. Now I'll see you in a minute." Zaylen replied.

"I love you too baby." I replied.

A bitch would have hit the Quan, hit the Nae Nae and all that shit. When you love somebody, and they loved you back, the feeling is indescribable. I had been praying they let me out, but the way my luck set up, they probably would lock my ass up and throw away the key.

It seemed like the time was moving slow as hell for me to go to court. Finally, they were coming to get me to transport me to court. When I made it in the courtroom, the first person, I saw was my mom. She gave me the warmest smile. Next to her was my baby Zaylen. He blew me a kiss and winked. This nigga was looking so damn good in his Armani suit. I told y'all this nigga was a boss. What was so crazy was he matched my fly.

I sat down next to my lawyer and she started briefing. You best believe Zaylen was right there listening. As she was talking to me, she was giving Zaylen a weird look. *I wonder what that's about* I thought to myself. While we were sitting there talking to my lawyer, in walked this clown Za'Kari. I wasn't going to lie, he came in looking like a whole snack, but fuck him. He sat on the other side looking directly at me. I wouldn't even look at his ass.

"All rise for the honorable Judge Nethercut." The bailiff yelled as the judge was walking in.

We all stood up. To be honest, my ass wanted to run up out that motherfucka. His ass came in that bitch looking like he hated black people. I looked at Zaylen and he mouthed *I love you. We got this.*

"I see here that the defendant chose to take a plea deal. Is this correct?" Judge Nethercut asked.

"Yes, your Honor." My attorney Shauntae answered.

"Ms. Steele, do you understand that you are pleading guilty and do you understand the charges?" Judge Nethercut asked.

"Yes, your Honor." I replied.

"Ms. Steele, I have gone over your case a million times. I even looked at your background. You have never been in trouble with the law and got good grades. You never even been kicked out of school. So, it puzzles me how you got caught up with drugs. You look like a very bright young lady, and I know you are not a threat to society. The only flaw you have is the not snitching rule that people go by today. So, I have no choice but to sentence you to five years with the possibility of parole in two years. I hope this teaches you to think about the company you keep. When you get out you still will have plenty of time to get back on the right track." Judge Nethercut said.

When he banged his gavel, the only thing I could remember is him saying five years with the possibility of parole in two. I couldn't believe my life had come to this. Never in a million years would I have thought that I would be going to prison and not to FAMU. What the fuck just happened?

I turned around and Za'Kari's bitch ass had his head down. The sorry ass excuse for a man couldn't even look at me. I couldn't look at my mama because I couldn't stand to see the disappointment on her face. Zaylen walked up to me and hugged me.

"Baby we got this. Don't you dare cry. Be strong I'll be up there every weekend to see you. Remember it's you and me against the world." Zaylen whispered in my ear.

I looked over at Za'Kari and he was mugging us. I mouthed to his ass I fucking hate you. I'm coming for yo ass so get ready bitch. When the officer put those cuffs around my wrists, I swear it felt like my life was over.

Chapter Twelve

Rhae

Four Years Later…

"Inmate Steele, you ready to get up out of this hell hole, because I'm tired of looking at your ass," My favorite CO Roderick said while laughing.

"You're tired of looking at me and I'm tired of being here with all this depressing shit," I said while folding my clothes and putting them in my bag.

I gave this place four long years of my life for some shit I didn't do. You just don't know how many times I wanted to give up and throw in the towel. I couldn't do that though because I had people on the outside waiting for me and rooting for me.

I looked at all the letters my baby wrote me, and he didn't miss not one week while I was here. He never missed a monthly visit either. Before I got locked up, I didn't have too many friends. The only friend I had was my so-called best friend Kazie. I thought she was my sister from another mister, but I later found out she was fucking my ex all along.

It wasn't like I was falling out with her over no nigga, because that's not it. The reason I felt betrayed was that was my boyfriend and it was plenty of nights I would call her phone crying about how Za'Kari was cheating and doggin' me out, and she would be the same bitch telling me to leave his no good ass. Now I see why because she was only giving me that advice so I could get out of the picture.

I swear the old me would fuck her up as soon as I seen her, but I was just going to let that bitch name karma deal with her ass. I had too many other things I needed to focus on like staying up out of here. I already received my GED while I was here since I couldn't graduate. I was going to enroll in Wayne State University for business management because I eventually wanted to open up a line of boutiques all through Detroit, before getting locked up that was one of my dreams.

"You almost done Inmate Steele, because at the rate you're moving, you will be here another night. You still have to go through processing and that will take a few hours." Roderick the CO said.

"Hell nah, I don't want to stay in this place another minute. I'm finished now." I said while grabbing my things.

I didn't even bother to look back to see if I left anything. If I left something oh well. I had the most important things in my bag. I made sure of it. Once I made it to processing, they gave me my bags so I could change my clothes. I put on the same thing I had when I came into this raggedy place.

I didn't know why, but I was getting nervous. I mean I had been locked in a cage for four long years. I knew things in the world have changed. I had been fucked over by two people I trusted and loved which made it hard for me to trust period. But I was going to leave all that negative shit in the past and look forward to my future.

Once they were done processing me, the CO walked me to the gate so I could leave.

"Don't come back to this hell hole. You didn't deserve to be here anyway. Just make better choices about the company you keep. Follow your heart and your dreams and stay far away from fuck boys." The CO said while unlocking the gate.

Once the gate was open, I saw Zaylen sitting on his all black Range looking all daddyish. For some reason it seemed like it was taking forever for me to get to him. He must have felt my presence because he looked up and started smiling. That smile put a little more pep in my step. Matter of fact, I threw my things on the ground and took off running. Once I reached him, I jumped in his arms and just started crying. You just don't know how long I have been waiting to hug this man outside those walls.

"Don't you start that crying, love. You know I don't like to see my baby cry." Zaylen said while putting me back on the ground and wiping my tears.

"I know baby, but I can't help it. I am just so happy to be out of that hell hole and to be in your arms." I said while looking in his eyes.

"I know I'm happy to see you too love, but you ain't about to have a real nigga out here crying. That's for damn sho." Zaylen said while going to get my things.

I had to laugh because men always try to hide their emotions. It was ok because I knew deep down inside, his ass was more sensitive than I was. After getting into the truck, I just laid my head back on the headrest and let my body get comfortable and enjoy the plush leather seats, because it was going to be a long four hour ride back to the D.

"Are you ready to go home, love?" Zaylen asked while starting the truck up and pulling out of the prison and grabbing my hand.

"As ready as I'll ever be." I said while smiling.

The ride home was smooth, and I slept like a baby. I woke up just as we were making our way downtown Detroit. I had no clue where we were going, but wherever we were going, I hoped my mama and little sisters were there because I missed them and couldn't wait to see them.

"Baby where are we going?" I asked while looking around.

"What you mean where we are going? We are going home love. I know you want to get out those old ass clothes and take a nice hot bubble bath. Don't worry that pretty little head of yours. Daddy got you." Zaylen said while bouncing his head to the new Drake.

As I looked around, there was a lot that had changed in the city. I guess the saying time waits for no man was true. I mean there were all kinds of businesses and condos being built everywhere. There was even a new arena for the Detroit Pistons. The last place I remember them playing was at the Palace of Auburn Hills.

I see I was going to have to learn my way around again because this is definitely not how I remember downtown looking. I made a mental note to myself to go to the Secretary of State building to get my license sometime this week, because I was not about to be getting chauffeured around by Zaylen.

I know he didn't mind, but I would never make the mistake of depending on another man to do anything for me when I could do things myself. I learned that there was nothing like your own. We pulled up to some nice condos on W. Lafayette. I mean they were nice with valet parking and all. Damn, I knew my baby was out here getting money, but I didn't know he was out here getting it like that.

When it was finally our turn, Zaylen pulled up to the valet, got out and came around to open my door. The sight alone had me in awe.

"Welcome home love." Zaylen said while opening the door for me.

I walked in and stood to the side so that he could lead the way. Hell I didn't know where I was going. He grabbed my hand and we walked through the lobby and passed the front desk. He used some card to give us access to the penthouse. Once we got off, we went to the only door on the floor, Zaylen used the same card to open the door.

"Surprise!" My mom and two little sisters Passion and Peaches yelled.

I ran to my mom and gave her the biggest hug ever. I missed her so much. It was not a day that went by that I didn't regret not listening to her. Nobody wanted to put their mom through that kind of pain and disappointment.

I was her first born and I was supposed to be a role model to my little sisters. Hell, it was just us. It was always been just us since my father left us, and as far as I was concerned, he could stay wherever the hell he was. My mother did a damn good job raising us on her own.

"There's my Rhae." My mother said while kissing me all over my face.

"Mama I missed you so much." I said while hugging her.

"Hey big sis. You need to let me get in that head of yours because you look real raggedy by the head." Peaches said while laughing.

"Oh, really? Well I'm definitely going to take you up on that offer as soon as I change these clothes." I said while sitting on the sofa.

"Aye family let me steal my baby for a few so that I can show her around and get her situated." Zaylen said while grabbing my hand.

"I'll be back down once I finish and Mama, I hope you cooked because I'm starving." I said while following Zaylen.

"Yes, baby I cooked all your favorites. Now go get situated we will be here when you're done."

Chapter Thirteen

"Next," I yelled to the next customer in line.

"Good afternoon sweetie." The old lady said to me while putting her items on the counter.

I don't know why old people got to be so fucking friendly. It was only so much smiling I could do. I had been standing up for six hours and I was ready to go home. I didn't know why God wouldn't bless me with a nigga with money so I could quit this dead-end ass Wal-Mart job.

I mean don't get me wrong it pays my bills, but it for damn sure not enough. I thought I had one in Za'Kari, but he turned out to be a bum ass selfish ass nigga. I still fucked with him from time to time but nothing serious. I regret the day I betrayed my only best friend Rhae. She was the only person that really cared about me. I was young and dumb back then and gone off that dope dick and jealously. If that nigga would have told me to betray Jesus himself, I probably would have.

I was always jealous of Rhae because she had all the things that I didn't have. She had the looks, a family, and she was smart as hell. Everybody loved Rhae from the old people in the neighborhood to the dope boys. I thought if I took something of hers, it would make me feel better about my fucked up life. I mean it did for a minute, but eventually reality set in and I was back to being depressed.

The only good thing I had going for myself was my apartment and my 2011 Impala that I just paid off. I didn't fuck with my mama because she acted more like a home girl than a parent and we argued and damn near came to blows every day. Thank God she was smart enough not to have any more kids. I hung out with a few girls from the neighborhood but I don't consider them to be my friends. I heard that Rhae was getting out soon. Hopefully she got over that bullshit that happened four years ago because I really missed my best friend. If I knew then what I knew now, things between us would have been different. I would have left Za'Kari's ass alone a long time ago. I thought he was going to be my come up, but all he left me with was a wet ass and an abortion.

Who the hell am I kidding? She still hadn't forgiven me. How I know is because every letter I wrote apologizing to her, was returned. I mean damn she knew Za'Kari wasn't shit. I just proved the theory to be true. If you ask me, I did her a favor. I gave her the push to leave him alone. On top of all that her and Zaylen's fine, well-paid ass was together now. Nobody was trippin' about that. I was supposed to be with him. No, we were never in a relationship, but we kicked it a few times. If she forgives me great, if she doesn't oh well at least I tried.

"Excuse me, are you okay honey?" The old lady being waited on asked.

"Nah she's not ok. Her ass looks like she high off something. I have been standing in this damn line for twenty minutes. She needs to hurry the hell up. People got shit to do. That's why I hate coming to Wal-Mart. Their customer service sucks." The ratchet girl yelled while rolling her eyes.

You see why I hate this job? People act like they don't have no home training. Everybody in America knows if you go to Wal-Mart you gone be in there for a minute. So why this dumb broad thought today was going to be any different, I have no clue. I snapped out of the trance I was in and started moving a little faster, because if this bitch said another word, I was liable to lose my fucking job.

As I waited on loud mouth, I heard a voice I hadn't heard in four years. I looked up and there Rhae was in my line with Zaylen. They were so busy being lovey dovey, they didn't even realize they were in my line.

"Baby I don't know why you wanted to come to Wal-Mart to get this shit. We could have gone to the mall to Victoria Secret or some shit. You don't have to be cheap. I knew I should have just had the girls go shopping for you." Zaylen said while kissing Rhae on the lips.

"What you mean I'm being cheap? Ain't nobody being cheap it's called saving money baby. Ain't nothing wrong with shopping at Wal-Mart. They have named brand shit, and you never let another woman shop for another woman's underwear fool." Rhae said while laughing.

"What's up Rhae? How long have been out?" I asked while grabbing her things to ring up.

"Oh, wow. There goes my good day. Why the fuck are you even talking to me? Oh, you thought because it's been four years, I was just going to sweep that disloyal shit under the rug? You lucky I don't fuck you up right here in this line. Yeah, I got your letters with your whack ass apologies and I still don't forgive you and never will. So, do us both a favor and don't speak to me when you see me. You're dead to me." Rhae said while walking away.

"Damn I guess baby told you, and please stay away from us, Kazie. You don't want these problems trust me." Zaylen said while paying for their things and walking away shaking his head.

Well damn that went well. I couldn't believe she was still tripping about some shit that happened four years ago. Then Zaylen's ass gon' have the nerve to threaten me. They really don't know who they were fucking with. I ain't going to lie. Rhae look damn good for her to have been locked up for four years. The bitch still had a better life than me.

I looked at the clock and it was time to go, so I turned my light out, emptied my draw and walked towards the back so I could clock out and leave. I decided to grab me a bite to eat from this wing place called Nikola's because I was tired and depressed and didn't feel like cooking.

I pulled into my assigned parking space, and I swear I wanted to turn around and go far away because Za'Kari's was sitting outside in his Tahoe waiting for me. I was so glad I took my damn key from his ass because if he had it, he would have been in my house and I really didn't feel like being bothered. I knew if I pulled off, he would have got mad and I didn't feel like arguing. So, I just grabbed my food and got out.

"What do you want Za'Kari? I am tired, and I really don't feel like being bothered." I said while walking right past his ass while he was getting out of his truck.

"Well hello to you too boo. What's with the attitude? Ain't you happy to see me? Za'Kari asked while grabbing my bags out my hand.

"Because people have been getting on my nerves all day. Starting with Wal-Mart customers on down to Rhae's ass." I said while rolling my eyes and unlocking my door.

"Wait did you just say Rhae? When did she get out?" Za'Kari said while smiling.

Look at this fool smiling like I just said told him he won the lottery or some shit. This bitch was really starting to get on my nerve. Everybody loved Rhae. What the fuck made her so damn special?

"I don't know why you over there smiling like you about to rekindle some shit, because her and your brother looked very happy. So, you might as well keep being the hoe that you are and go on about your life. Ain't you the reason she lost four years of her life?" I asked while sitting down so I could eat my food.

"I ain't trying to rekindle shit. I mean damn, I can't be happy she's out? You know you always have been jealous of Rhae. I used to tell her that shit too. Let me move around before I forget you're a female and smack the fuck out of you!" Za'Kari said while walking to the door to leave.

I guess he thought that little tantrum he just had was supposed to make me mad. I could give two fucks about his feelings or anybody else's at this point. I was tired of Rhae's ass already and the bitch ain't even been free for a whole week. I mean if it wasn't for me, her ass wouldn't even be with Zaylen's fine ass because she would still be stuck on stupid about Za'Kari's ass. She got a lot of nerve having a fucked-up attitude when I helped her ass out. Shit I was the one out here still struggling. She got out of prison and didn't have to worry about shit.

Shit something had to give. I needed to knock that bitch off her high horse. As I was eating, a thought popped into my head. Everybody knew Shauntae and Zaylen were a thing back in the day, and that Shauntae wasn't wrapped too tight when it came to Zaylen. I know she felt some type of way when she found out that Rhae wasn't really Za'Kari's girlfriend but Zaylen's and she helped her. I picked up my phone so I could Google the address to her law office. It looked like I would be making a trip downtown Monday. A woman who is still in love with a man and feels played, is a dangerous woman. Let the games begin.

Chapter Fourteen

Za'Kari

I was going over Kazie's house to chill and get my dick wet, but after finding out my baby was out, those thoughts went out the window, literally. It wasn't a day that went by that I didn't think about her and how I fucked her over. That girl was down for me. Any and everything I asked her to do, she did with no questions asked. I know I fucked up, but everybody made mistakes. Shit nobody was saying shit about her fucking with my blood brother. I know she was hurt and mad about the shit I did, but you didn't get a nigga back like that. I couldn't believe she was out already. Those years went by fast.

I know she was still mad because I wrote her so many times and she still had yet to respond to at least one. I know it was the right information because I got the information from Shauntae's ass. I know she still loved me because I was her first everything. Plus, I was not the same man I was four years ago. Everybody changes. Plus, my operation is up and running smoothly, and I don't need her to do anything, but sit up and spend my money. I hadn't been in a real relationship since Rhae. All these hoes could get from me was a quick fuck. Hell they couldn't even get a kiss on the lips. Only lips I wanted to kiss for the rest of my life was Rhae's. Damn I missed my baby. Why is it you never realize what a good thing you have until you lose it? I planned on getting her back, even if it meant getting rid of my hoe ass brother.

I decided to go and check on my OG since I hadn't checked on her in a while and I needed to make my payment for the loan she gave me to pay off Winston's ass. It was sad I had to borrow the money from my OG, when I know my punk ass brother or my daddy could have just given me the money really but fuck it. It was what it was. I really didn't like to go around my OG like that because she was always trying to get me to talk to my brother, but that shit would never happen. This nigga had no clue what the word loyalty meant. He took my bitch, and he didn't help me when I was beefing with Winston's bitch ass. So, fuck Zaylen and whoever else was riding for that nigga. He could be right in front of my face on fire and I probably would throw gasoline on his ass. I know people were probably thinking it was a little harsh speaking about my brother like that, but shit blood don't make us family.

I pulled up to my OG's house and there was a black on black Range sitting in the driveway. I wonder who the hell this could be because my OG didn't fuck with too many people since she had trust issues. I checked my hip to make sure I had my shit on me. I know I should have called before coming, but this was my mama, I shouldn't have too. I got out my Cadillac Escalade and walked up to the Range, so I could look inside to see if I could get a clue who it was. Call me nosey if you want too, I really didn't care. It wasn't like I was popping up to some random females house. When I leaned on the window to look inside, the damn alarm went off.

Ole sensitive ass alarm. Damn now they were gonna know I was looking all in their shit. Before I could even move away, my OG's front door flew open. I swear I stopped breathing because standing right in front of me was the love of my life. Damn she looked damn good too. She lost her baby fat and was thick in all the right places, and you could still get lost in her gray eyes. Her skin was flawless and glowing. I had to swallow because I really didn't know what to say or what to do at this moment. She must have felt the same way because she had the same reaction.

By the time I finally got my thoughts together, she was moving toward the truck. I didn't want to let her leave. I mean I had been waiting four years to even be in the same room as Rhae. I had to think fast because I could not let this opportunity pass me up, so I grabbed her by the arm before she could get into the truck.

"Damn Rhae baby. It's like that? We can't have a conversation like adults?" I asked while still holding her arm.

"Get your hands off of me Za'Kari before I cut that motherfucka off! I don't got shit to say to you at all, and I am not trying to disrespect your mother's house." Rhae replied while snatching her arm away.

"Rhae I know you are not still tripping about that shit that happened four years ago? It looks like you survived. Now we can move past all that shit and get back to us." I said while trying to grab her hand again.

"Wow I see nothing has changed about you at all Za'Kari. You still think I am some weak bitch that is just going to listen to your bullshit. Well correction dumbass, I am not the same little dumbass girl anymore! I learned from my mistakes. I don't know how you could even fix your lips to even speak to me after the shit you put me through. You're lucky I don't have a gun because I probably would blow your big ass head off. Get back to us? Nigga, it stopped being us when I heard the doors lock on the jail cell. I worked so hard to graduate and make my mama proud, but I couldn't even let her see me walk across that stage because I had to serve time for a nigga that don't care about nobody but his damn self. To make shit worse, you fucked my best friend and had a whole relationship with her. So, please explain to me how you even thought, in that fucked up head of yours that there could or would be an us? Like I told your girl, stay the fuck away from around me or I'm liable to go to jail for some shit that I did do!" Rhae said while walking around me.

I mean she moved so fast that I couldn't even plead my case. I didn't think I liked this new Rhae. She was far from the dumb little broad that did everything I told her to do. No, this Rhae was confident and not taking no bullshit. Maybe if she had that attitude, she wouldn't have served that time. A person would only do what you allowed them to do. She was going to listen to me. I didn't give a fuck who she thought she was now. I went to the driver's side of the Range and I yanked it open and snatched her ass out.

"Za'Kari what the fuck are you doing?" Rhae yelled while kicking trying to break free.

"Za'Kari you put that damn girl down now. You can't make nobody talk to you." My OG said while grabbing my arms.

"Ma I am not going to hurt her at all. I just want to talk to her. That's it." I said while holding Rhae in a bear hug and walking her towards my truck.

"I am not going anywhere with you Za'Kari!' Rhae yelled while still kicking and screaming.

"You can stop fighting me because you are going to listen to what the fuck I have to say. Don't act like you don't remember how I get down." I said while putting her in the car and putting on the child lock so she couldn't get out.

"Za'Kari you know damn well you're wrong! You basically took four years of that girl's life that she can't get back, and here you are trying to force your way back into her life. I thought you were a little off, but I see you are just plain crazy.

How in the hell would you feel if somebody did what you did to her to me?" My OG said while shaking her hand.

"Ma you know damn well you would have never been put into this situation. You knew better. Plus, you know me and Zaylen are not playing that shit about you period. Everybody acts like Rhae is innocent in all this. Let's not forget that she is in a relationship with my blood brother. I don't hear you saying nothing about that. You always treated him better. I had her first. Believe it or not, I love this girl. Do you know I haven't been in a serious relationship since she been locked up? So, I don't give a fuck what you or anybody else says or thinks, she is mine. I don't give a fuck if I have to make you lose a son. I'm taking back what the fuck belongs to me!" I said while walking around and getting into the truck and pulling off, leaving my OG standing in the middle of the driveway.

Rhae was on the passenger side calling me everything but the child of God. Like I said, she was going to hear what the fuck I had to say. I know

Zaylen was going to be worried and try to find her. That was why I took her iPhone and turned it off. I don't need any interruptions. My OG stayed right by The Lodge Freeway so I hopped on there and headed towards downtown to Belle Isle where it all began for us. It didn't take us long to make it there because there wasn't any traffic at all. I guess Rhae realized that I wasn't letting her go until she talked to me because she was sitting in the passenger seat with a mug on her face, looking out the window. I wanted to laugh because she looked like a big ass baby pouting and shit. I pulled up to a parking space in front of the water. At first, I just sat there staring at the water. I guess I was making Rhae even more irritated because she was huffing and puffing.

"Look Rhae, I know what I did was fucked up and we can't get that time back, but I really do apologize for how everything played out. How was I supposed to know that the feds were watching? You really think if I knew they were watching I would have still been running my operation through your house? The reason I let you take the fall because you know I have a record and the judge would have thrown the book at my ass. I would have done more than four years. To be honest, I didn't even think that they were going to give you any time at all. You just don't know how I felt when Judge Nethercut sentenced you. It was like all my air left my body. I kept money on your books, and I wrote you every day. So, don't sit here acting like it was all bad because it wasn't." I said while touching her cheek.

All of a sudden, she started laughing with tears running down her face. I don't know if she was crying from laughing so hard or if she just lost her damn mind. Whatever she was going through, I at least owe her that much. So, I just waited to see what she was going to do next.

"Is that why you kidnapped me so that you could tell me that bullshit? You can't be fucking serious right now Za'Kari. You just really can't be serious right now. Do you understand how much you fucked up my life? I have fucking nightmares about being locked up. I have trust issues, and you turned my fucking heart cold. I can't even love the people who deserve my love the right way because I am scared that they are going to betray me. I fucking hate you and if I wasn't so terrified of going back to jail, the first day out I would have found you and killed your ass. You were my everything. Nigga, I lost my fucking virginity to you. You were supposed to be my first and my last. So, excuse the fuck out of me if I seem a little bitter. Thank God for Zaylen. If it wasn't for him, ain't no telling where my dysfunctional ass would be. Loyalty and love kept me in some situations that common sense should have got me out of. Now take me back to your mom's so I can get my vehicle and get back to my man and family." Rhae yelled.

She still didn't understand that I loved her and I was not letting her go that fucking easy. She would eventually see that back then I was young and dumb and had no clue what the fuck I was doing. I know she lost some years, but she was young. She still had time to get her shit together. I didn't know why she thought Zaylen was any better than me. I know he wasn't faithful to her while she was locked up. If I could just prove to her that he was disloyal, then she would drop his ass. I was not going to address me sleeping with Kazie because that shit was irrelevant. If anything, she should be mad at is Kazie's ass. She was the one who came on to me. Tired of going back and forth, I decided to just take her back to her car so I could figure out how the hell I was going to get it through her thick skull that I was who she was supposed to be with.

"Look I am going to take you back to your car, but just know I ain't going nowhere and you will always be mine." I said while backing out the parking space and heading back to the lodge freeway.

"Whatever just give me my damn phone before Zaylen puts an APB out on me." Rhae said while snatching her iPhone out my hand.

As soon as I was about to say something, someone banged us hard as hell from the back, as I was trying to pull over to the side of the road, they rammed me again.

"What the fuck is going on Za'Kari? Who the fuck is trying to run us off the road? Don't tell me it's one of your hoes!" Rhae screamed while looking back.

'I don't have no motherfuckin' hoes. I don't know who the fuck it is!" I yelled back while trying to control the truck.

I finally pulled over and the car that was ramming us got over too. Oh I see this motherfucka got balls. I put the car in park and jumped out with my shit pointed at the truck. The windows were tinted so dark that I couldn't see on the inside. Once I made it to the vehicle, I used the end of my gun to bust out the driver side window.

"What the fuck?" I yelled at the driver.

Chapter Fifteen

Rhae

I was just going over to Ms. Washington's to drop off some documents for Zaylen. When I got there, she was cooking her famous chicken wings with the lemon pepper. I couldn't resist. Before I even made my way over to her place, I asked her was Za'Kari going to be coming to visit today and she told me that he really doesn't come over because he didn't want to run into Zaylen. So, I figured it would be safe to visit. In the middle of me eating, I heard the alarm on my truck go off. Once I made it to the door, I already knew who it was when he had his back turned. Of course, he wanted to explain why he did what he did, and of course I wasn't listening to the bullshit.

Now I am here on the side of the road with whiplash because one of Za'Kari's crazy ass females tried to run us off the road. I sat my ass right in the car because this shit had nothing to do with me, and I was not the one she even needed to be worried about, trust me. I guess you could say curiosity got the best of me, because my nosey ass turned around in the front seat. I swear the broad looked like my attorney Shauntae. When I looked a little closer it was her. *Don't tell me she fucking Za'Kari too* I thought to myself. I turned back around and was about to send a text and all of a sudden, I heard a loud crash on my side of the truck. Oh, this bitch done lost her damn mind I mumbled to myself. I then climbed over to the driver side and got out.

"Why the fuck would you do that knowing someone was on the passenger side? I could have gotten glass in my eye or anything. I hope you are not showing your ass because you think Za'Kari and I got something going on, because honey all you had to do was just ask me. Za'Kari and I are nothing. He is just a piece of my past that I wish I could erase. I don't want him. Trust me I don't. I have a man and he's at home waiting on me. So I am just going to act like you did not just bust the passenger side window while I was sitting there, because you got bigger problems to worry about, like how to get this lame nigga out your life before he ruins it like he did mine. Za'Kari, don't worry about taking me back to my vehicle. I'll catch a Lyft." I said while pulling up the Lyft app on my phone.

"Nah I meant to do that. I wish I could have knocked your fucking head off. If I knew then what I know now, I would have made a few calls and your ass would still be in jail. I can't believe I helped the enemy. All this time I thought you were with Za'Kari when you really were with my man Zaylen. Well bitch I am here to let you know we have history, and I am not letting him go." Shauntae said while swinging her Louisville slugger and mugging me.

Now I was confused. I thought she was just my attorney. I had no clue that this broad was fucking Zaylen. No wonder why she was spazzing out. She felt like she had been played. At the end of the day, I was a woman first, so I could only imagine how she felt. Hell I basically went through the same thing with Za'Kari and Kazie's ass. One thing I would not tolerate was disrespect period. I know she was all in her feelings right now, but in my defense I had no clue about her and Zaylen's so called relationship. I had been locked up for four years. I know she didn't know about me or I wouldn't be sitting up here in this fucked up ass situation again over another nigga.

What the fuck was I thinking? I thought Zaylen was different, but as you can see the apple doesn't fall too far from the tree. I just wanted to be by myself and focus on getting my shit together. All this drama over a nigga was not even worth it. I was gonna mess around and end up in jail for life due to me killing some damn body. So, to avoid any of that, I was just going to remove myself from the situation.

"Look Shauntae, I am not sure what is going on between you and Zaylen, but woman to woman we have been together for the last four years. From what he told me, he had been single for a while. So if y'all was a happy couple, I wasn't aware and had I known, I would have fell back. I know what it feels like to be betrayed by a no-good ass nigga who you gave your heart too. But you mad at the wrong people. You should be trying to release that frustration and aggression towards Zaylen. I'm not going to lie, he's about to catch these hands for playing with my heart once again."

"Bitch you not about to put your hands on no motherfuckin' body. Stay the fuck away from Zaylen and this is the last time I'm going to tell you. Za'Kari you better get your bitch and you better tell this bitch about me". Shauntae said while walking back to her car.

Did this bitch just read me like that? I hadn't even been out of jail for thirty days and I was already about to go back in. I should have known this nigga was fucking this bitch because what nigga gone really pay attorney fees for a female, he barely knew? I blamed myself for allowing another person get close to me. I got something for all these motherfuckas. I wasn't going to even address

Zaylen about this bitch. I was just going to get my shit and go to my mom's place until I could get myself together. It said my Lyft driver was about three minutes away, which I was glad because Lord knows I needed to get the hell from around here.

"Rhae where the fuck do you think you about to go with a damn Lyft driver? These people crazy out here." Za'Kari said while walking towards me.

"Wow people out here crazy? You got a lot of nerve when you are one of the crazy people that you are talking about. I'm probably safer with them then your ass. I'm good. You don't have to worry about me. I'm a grown ass woman". I said while getting in my Lyft.

I was going to go back and get the truck, but I didn't even feel like seeing Zaylen right now. So, I just changed my destination and went towards my mom's house. I just need peace right now. That's it. We weren't far from my old neighborhood, and it felt good to be back, but it also reminded me of all the bullshit I had been through. We pulled up to my mom's and all I could do was smile, because my mom was the realest one on my team and I missed her and my little sisters so much.

I got out of the Lyft, completed my ride on my phone and walked to the front door and walked in. As I was walking up to the door, I could smell my mother's famous smothered potatoes. I was happy as hell, but at the same time, in my feelings because nobody called me and invited me over. The door was unlocked as usual. I don't know why but nobody ever did anything to our house. I walked in and walked straight to the kitchen.

"Ma you weren't going to call and tell me that you were cooking today? I feel left out." I said while walking up to my mom and kissing her on the cheek.

"Girl you better say something when you come in the house. You scared the hell out of me". My mom said while grabbing her chest."

"Now how the hell did I scare you when you know nobody is going to run up in here"? I said while looking into the pots on the stove.

"Rhaelyn, I know you know better to go into my pots without washing your hands, and where is Zaylen? I can't believe he let you out of his sight,". My mom said while stirring the food in the pots on the stove.

I rolled my eyes because just hearing that niggas name had me irritated to the point where if he was standing in front of me right now, I would smack the shit out of his ass.

"Oh lawd, it's trouble in paradise already? What done happened now child of mine?". My mom said while walking to the kitchen table and having a seat.

Not the one to tell my business, I decided to ignore my mom's question and go check on my little sisters. My mom already thought that Zaylen is a saint and right now, I don't even know what I am going to do about the situation with him and Shauntae, so it would be pointless to tell her what happened. Speaking of the devil my phone was ringing and vibrating in my hand, and I hit the ignore button. He called back again and got the same results. If he called back again, his ass was going to get blocked. I didn't know why people called you back to back like you didn't hear them calling the first time. I decided to check on my sisters once I woke up from my nap.

I walked in my old bedroom and it was exactly how I left it four years ago. I sat on the bed and looked around. There were even pictures of me, Kazie, and Za'Kari. As I looked at the pictures closer, they did look a little too close if you ask me. I guess all the signs were looking at me dead in my face I just didn't notice them. Enough about my past, I left that bullshit in that jail cell. Right now, I was just going to focus on moving forward. I had goals and dreams and I would accomplish every single one. I decided to throw all the pictures away because I would never have anything to do with either one of them, so what's the point in keeping memories. It was crazy how a person could do you wrong yet try to force their way back into your life like you did them wrong. Everybody had me so fucked up and I wish they would just leave me alone. I didn't get this much attention four years ago. I was just going to lay my ass down and go to sleep and figure out what I am going to do then.

Chapter Sixteen

Zaylen

I had called this crazy ass girl four times, and she didn't answer not one time nor had she called me back. She was just supposed to be going over to my OG's house to drop off some paperwork along with picking up some of my OG's famous hot wings. That was hours ago. I knew Za'Kari wasn't over there because before I even allowed her to go by herself, I called my OG and she told me that Z didn't come by unless he called first. I know she was not anywhere near Kazie's disloyal ass, so where the fuck could she be? I tried to ping her location but apparently her slick ass turned it off. I was not an insecure ass nigga. I was a man who was worried about his woman. There was all type of shit going on out here in these streets. I mean they were snatching our black women up on a regular and shipping them off. So, hell yeah, I was trying to figure out where the hell my woman was.

I was not the type of nigga to just sit around and do nothing, so I got out of my comfortable ass California King bed and hopped in the shower. After taking care of my hygiene and brushing my waves to perfection, I threw on my baby blue Nike joggers with my white and baby blue Nike t-shirt and my Detroit Lions hat. I finished off my fit with my crispy white air force ones straight out the box. I don't know why this woman wanted to test me like this. She knew I don't play no games. Before I could make it out the door my phone started ringing. I looked at the screen and saw that it was Shauntae. I really didn't feel like dealing with her shenanigans today, but me being me, I answered.

"What's up Shauntae? I'm kind of busy right now, so if this ain't a matter of life and death, then I am going to have to hit you back later," I said while making my way out of the house.

"Nah whatever you doing can wait. Your ass been avoiding me since I helped your little thot ass girlfriend four years ago, which I swear to God if I knew then what I found out after the bitch was sentenced, she would be up under the motherfuckin' jail. I can't believe you played me like that after everything we have been through. On top of that, she's your blood brother's GIRLFRIEND! What the fuck she loving the crew? That's the bitch you call yourself loving?" Shauntae said while rolling her eyes.

"First of all I'm going to need you to take that aggression out of your motherfuckin' voice. Second of all, we not together so if I wanted to fuck your best friend, I could do it. Who the fuck gone check me? Just what the fuck I thought. As far as playing you, that's a got damn lie. Let's not forget I retained you as my attorney and you represent whoever the fuck, I want you to represent as long as I pay your money hungry ass! You didn't even do a good job because my baby still did some time. So, you could miss me with all this bullshit that's coming out of your mouth. Like I said if it ain't life or death I'll hit you back." I said while getting in my Audi A7.

"Damn this bitch done gave you some of that prison pussy now you acting brand new. You being loyal to a bitch that can give two fucks about you. She was just with your brother a few hours ago. I know because on my way home from work, I was riding down Jefferson and guess who I see? Your so called bitch with your brother looking all in love and shit. Looks like you been played love. I guess you thought you could buy her love and loyalty. You should know better than that these hoes ain't loyal. So why you over there trying to take up for your so-called woman she probably busting it open for a real nigga." Shauntae said while taking a sip of her Pink Moscato.

"Look Shauntae, like I said I got shit to do. I bet you couldn't wait to run and tell me what the fuck you saw, thinking that shit was going to get you back in my bed. Well guess what it's not. I still don't want your miserable ass. Now get the fuck off my phone." I said before hanging up on her ass.

I'm not going to sit here and say that the little information that Shauntae just told me didn't have me on tip because I was on 1000, but I wasn't going to give her miserable ass the satisfaction of knowing that I was feeling some kind of way about Rhae being with my brother. Just thinking about this shit had me ready to kill both of their asses and throw their bodies in the Detroit River.

What I was trying to figure out is why she is even having a conversation with this nigga let alone in the car with him. I never would understand why and how someone could forgive a motherfucka who did them dirty. I felt like once a snake always a snake.

Before I go the fuck off, I am going to investigate the situation because sometimes looks could be deceiving. I tried calling Rhae's phone one more time, but it went straight to voicemail. What the fuck is she doing that she had to block me? This shit was beginning to look real suspect to me. I decided to call my OG since that's where her ass was supposed to be in the first damn place. The phone rang a few times before she answered.

"Yes, child of mine."

"Hey, Ma. What took you so long to answer the phone?" I asked while merging onto I 96.

"Child I was washing dishes and I couldn't find the dry towel. Anyway boy what do want?" My mom said while smacking her lips.

"I was calling to see if Rhae's ass was still over there because I have been trying to call her phone and it keeps going straight to voicemail." I asked while driving.

"No, she left here with Za'Kari. Not by choice though. He forced her into his truck and pulled off. I told him to leave that girl alone, but he insisted that he had to talk to her and that he wasn't going to hurt her. I was going to give him a little while longer and then I was going to call him. I don't think he would hurt her. He knows what will happen if he does.

"So let me get this straight. You know your son is not wrapped too tight and you allowed him to take my girl, and on top of all that, you didn't even call me to give me a heads up? You know what Ma, don't even worry about I'll find her, but I know one thing if he does anything to Rhae, you are going to have one less son."

Now I would never hang up on my mama, because to be honest that shit is disrespectful, but today she pissed me off. She was trying to keep the peace between my brother and me, but what she fails to understand is we would never have peace because we both loved Rhae. I really don't give a fuck about because Za'Kari was one selfish individual and he don't give a fuck about anyone but himself. I knew Rhae's worth and they didn't make them like her anymore. You think I am going to be a fool and let her go.

I reversed my Audi so I could head over to Za'Kari's house, because that was the only place that I could think of that they could be. I don't know why but my adrenaline was pumping, and I was preparing myself for the worst. Shit you couldn't blame me for the way I was feeling. Shit just wasn't adding up. Why would my woman be over her ex's house and why does she have me blocked? Thinking about the possibilities had me speeding down the Lodge Freeway like a bat out of hell. I made it to Za'Kari's house in no time. I grabbed my burner because I hadn't talked to my brother since the day of Rhae's court date, and I really didn't know where his mind is right now.

I pulled my burner out and banged on the door like I was DPD. I didn't give a fuck about cracking his glass on his front door either fuck him and his door.

"Why the fuck you pulling up to my shit without calling and banging on my door like you DPD or the Feds? What the fuck do you want?" Za'Kari asked while mugging me like I was some bum ass nigga off the street.

I had to laugh first before responding to his lame ass standing in front of me right now. He knew damn well he was not about that life for real.

"Bruh you can calm that tough shit down because we both know what it is. I am going to ask you this question one time and one time only. Where is Rhae?" I asked while waiting for some slick shit to come out of his mouth.

"What the fuck you mean where is Rhae? How the fuck would I know? She ain't my bitch. You stole her, remember? My own fucking blood brother. It was supposed to be bros before hoes."

One thing about me was I was very big on respect, and Za'Kari knows this. That's exactly why I shot his ass in the leg and then punched his ass in the throat. What type of nigga would I be if I didn't defend my Queen? Rhae was mine and I would be damned if I let any motherfuckin' body disrespect her, point blank period. This nigga was just talking real tough a few seconds ago, now he rolling on the ground hollering like a little bitch. I walked right over his disrespectful ass and walked right into his spot looking for my baby. I wasn't worried about Za'Kari at all because he was a little injured at the moment. I looked all through the house and she wasn't there. By the time I made it back downstairs, the paramedics and the pigs were helping Za'Kari's crybaby ass. "Are you Zaylen?" The officer asked.

"I'm sure you know the answer to that. What's up?" I asked while mugging Za'Kari. I know this nigga did not call the fucking pigs on me. That nigga knew he was a straight bitch. He knew damn well that you don't get the pigs involved in no street shit.

"Where is the gun that you shot the victim with?" The officer asked with his hand on his gun.

"Behind my back." I said while putting my hands up. Shit the way these pigs were killing us out here, ain't no way in hell I was about to reach for nothing behind my back. That would be giving them a reason to kill my ass.

I wasn't tripping anyway because my shit was registered, and it really was Za'Kari's word against mine. My record was clean, and my new lawyer Fieger was one of the top defense lawyers in the D. My only problem was I still don't know where the fuck Rhae was.

Chapter Seventeen

Shauntae

I couldn't believe after all the shit that me and Zaylen had been through, he played me for a nobody ass bitch. I had been stalking this nigga for years and I have never seen this bitch at all. So, I was trying to figure out where the fuck she came from. I mean I know she used to be Za'Kari's girlfriend. I was just trying to figure out where and how they developed a fucking relationship.

All this time I was been thinking the nigga was a down low brother, but instead his ass was in a relationship with one of my client's. The one he paid for me to represent. Talking about a bitch being fooled. Had I known that she was his little side piece, I would have made sure the little bitch was put under the jail. Shit I had seen people do football numbers for a couple of pounds of weed. This dumb bitch had cocaine being sent to her house, and she only got five to ten and the bitch only did four.

Thinking about the shit had me going crazy. I had to pull out some of my exotic and my papers. I broke the buds down and just had scooped the weed up to put it in my paper and my damn doorbell rang.

I looked at the door like the person on the other side could see me looking at them. Who the fuck could be knocking at my door? It was only a few people that knew where I stayed. I was a defense attorney and sometimes I didn't get my clients what they wanted. I didn't know if they would try to retaliate.

I grabbed my 9mm off the table stand drawer next to my sofa. I had guns all over my place. All I could say was let a motherfucka try me. I promise I was not going down without somebody going down with me. That was one thing Zaylen taught me. Always stay strapped and always know your surroundings.

I made it to the door and looked out the peephole and it was the last person I wanted to see.

The devil is really busy today, because the Lord knows how I felt about Za'Kari's ass. I knew I was going to regret it later, but I opened the door.

"What do you want Za'Kari?" I asked while walking over to the bar. I needed two shots of Patron.

"Don't answer the door with that punk ass 9 and a fucked-up ass attitude, because you knew I was coming after the shit you pulled yesterday. Yo duck head ass broke the windows out my shit like you my bitch and you caught me cheating or some shit. You know you are about to reimburse me for that shit right now too, but we will discuss that before I leave. So, who told you about your disloyal ass ex talking to my girl? Let me guess Kazie's ass called you? She always was jealous of Rhae, but that shit doesn't matter. What are we going to do to break they asses up? Because I got plans for Rhae. I need my bitch back like yesterday! You see how fine she is? I mean she fine and thick as fuck. Jail got my baby looking scrumptious." Za'Kari said while licking his lips.

"Unt Unt nobody wants to hear that shit Za'Kari. That bitch ain't all that, and what the fuck happen to your leg?" I asked while throwing my shot back.

"Zaylen's bitch ass shot me in the leg yesterday, because I called Rhae out her name and he thought she was over my house. Matter fact, I should slap the fuck out your crazy ass. All this bullshit didn't start happening until you followed us yesterday. Yo ass is the fucking devil. Now what the hell are we going to do about our little situation because we are both miserable right now and I need some love and affection." I just looked at his dumb ass like he was crazy. He always had been dramatic. I swear he and Zaylen were like night and day.

"What do you mean what are we going to do about our situation? You were just with the bitch. Why didn't you put your foot down and tell her that the shit with Zaylen is over? Ohhh she doesn't want your crazy ass! I wouldn't either after yo ass done had me locked up for four years for some shit that I had nothing to do with! Did you really have drugs mailed to that girl's house for real? "I said while laughing and taking another shot.

"I guess we are one in the same because Zaylen for damn sure don't want your ass either, and hasn't for years ever since you killed my niece or nephew. While you're crazy ass sitting over there laughing and shit. You knew my brother had you and his seed, but we both know why you had an abortion. You didn't know if it was his or the next nigga. I know all about you being the neighborhood hoe. Just admit we both have done some fucked up shit to people. So, I know you got something brewing in that evil ass head of yours. All I'm saying is I want in."

"Fuck you Za'Kari and stop bringing up old shit! All I know is the bitch got to go. I don't care if you have to kidnap her ass and take her to another fucking country. Matter of fact that doesn't sound like a bad idea, or we could set her up and send her ass back to jail for life."

"You know what you have always been a selfish motherfucka this is not just about you. You or nobody else is going to touch Rhae, and she is not going back to jail. How about I just kill Zaylen and that will solve everything!" Za'Kari yelled.

"I know you better quit yelling at me, and you better not touch Zaylen."

"Don't sit up here and act like my brother can't be touched because trust me, he can. Now what's the damn plan and I need the money for the damages your crazy ass did to my damn truck."

"I'm not giving you shit Za'Kari. You shouldn't have had the bitch in your car." I replied.

"Oh, you're going to pay me my money or I'm going to fuck it out of you. Your choice. I know you remember what this dick feels and taste like, don't you?" Za'Kari asked while licking his lips and standing in front of me. Got damn it why the hell he got to be so fine and with a big dick? I had not had a real orgasm in about a year, and I knew if anybody could make that happen, it was definitely Za'Kari's fine ass. Shit Zaylen's fucking his girlfriend so why not? I dropped the robe I had on to the floor and slowly walked over to where Za'Kari was sitting and got down on my knees. I unzipped his pants and unleashed the beast. Za'Kari had one of those pretty dicks. You know the ones that made you want to put the whole ten inches down your throat, not caring if you choke or not. I slowly put each inch in my mouth while giving him eye contact. The more I put into my mouth, the better it tasted. Once I got comfortable with all ten inches in my mouth, I went crazy sucking and licking making sure I kept my mouth wet. Za'Kari liked it sloppy. He liked to see the drool coming out of the side of my mouth. I must have been doing a good job because his eyes were rolling in the back of his head like he was having a seizure.

After sucking the soul out of his body, Za'Kari picked me up and put me on the wall with my legs in his arms. He then opened my pussy lips with his tongue and started licking and biting gently on my clit. Jesus take the wheel because the way this man is eating my pussy right now, I was liable to marry his ass. He then started fucking me with his tongue going in and out in and out. I tried to control my orgasm but that wasn't possible, because it was like he knew every spot to lick and suck on, which made the water works come. I wasn't even done recovering from the orgasm I just had from him eating my pussy, wheb he just put me right down on his dick. I fucking screamed because it hurt so good, if that made sense. Za'Kari fucked me all over my house for hours. I lost count of how many orgasms this man has made me have.

After that dope dick, I was ready to take my ass to sleep, but apparently Za'Kari's ass still wanted to talk about getting his girl back. I mean, me personally I don't know how this nigga could be thinking about another bitch when he just had the best sex his ass probably could ever have. Shit I forgot about Zaylen's ass that quick. I guess the bitch was out here putting spells on these niggas, because I couldn't even get one to love me. What the hell. I got up with an attitude feeling exactly how I felt before I got dicked down. I got out the bed and went into my bedroom and slammed the bathroom door.

"Get the fuck out now Za'Kari. I hate your stupid ass!" I yelled from the other side of the door.

"Oh, you thought because you gave me the pussy and that good head that it was going to make me forget about my baby? Nah sweetheart, see nobody will ever take Rhae's place. I just needed to get this nut off. I still don't like your bougie ass. You're not my type".

"Fuck you Za'Kari. I said get the fuck out. I don't care that I am not your type, nor do I give a fuck about taking that ratchet ass bitches place. All I know is she better leave Zaylen alone before she ends up back in jail." I yelled while turning on the shower. I must have hit a nerve because my bathroom door was being kicked in and Za'Kari snatched my little ass up by the throat. I swear I saw my life flash before my eyes.

"Let me tell you this shit one last time. Nothing and I mean nothing is going to happen to Rhae, so you better rethink whatever fucked up plan you got going on in that fucked up head of yours when it comes to that one. Now call me when you come up with a plan that doesn't include doing shit to my baby. I am going to leave you alone to think about the master plan. I'll be back for some of that wet ass pussy and that phenomenal head. I taught you well." Zakarri replied while still holding me by the throat.

He dropped me like I was a sack of potatoes. I wanted to trip his ass, but I knew if I did that shit, he would beat my ass so I took the smart route and just let his ass leave. I didn't care what nobody said, or how many threats I received about this bitch, she got to go like yesterday. I don't know where this little bitch came from, but she was the one that is interfering with my happiness. She had the hearts of the men I wanted and loved, and I always got my way.

Chapter Eighteen

Rhae

I needed that nap. I decided to get up and eat because my stomach was growling. I don't know what made me go to sleep without eating, and I guess I was just that irritated. I guess Zaylen was out doing him because when I looked at my phone there were no missed calls from him at all. Oh well I wasn't going to stress myself about a nigga that wasn't stressing over me. A nigga would tell you everything you wanted to hear and then when they get you under their spell, that's when they want to show you their true colors. I went down to the kitchen and all the food was put away and the kitchen was clean. I really didn't feel like cleaning up the kitchen. Good thing my mama loved me because she had made me a plate so all I had to do is put in the microwave and viola, magic.

After stuffing my face with my mama's delicious cooking, I decided to go and ask my mama if I could borrow her car so that I could head downtown and get the rest of my things. Hopefully Zaylen was out doing God know what, because right now, I really don't want to see him at all. I ran upstairs and knocked on mama's door.

"Come in whichever one of my girls it is." My mom replied while watching her Fox 2 News. I swear this lady stayed watching the news to see who she knows, which probably is everybody because she is well known around the D.

"Hey ma. I was wondering if I could borrow your car to go get my things from Zaylen's house. I think I am going to stay here for a while until I can get myself together." I replied while sitting in the recliner chair in her room.

"Oh Lord. Get your things from Zaylen's house? I thought it was your house too. What could have happened in a couple of hours that would make you want to move back home? I mean don't get me wrong, I don't mind and you are always welcomed, but baby I didn't raise you to run away from your problems. I raised you to face them head on. You don't have to tell me, but I know that Zaylen loves you because of his actions. There is no man out here that would do the things he has done for you if he didn't love you. Just think about that before you make these drastic decisions and be out here lonely and heartbroken." My mom said while getting up to had me her car keys.

I hated when my mama could read me like that, but she was right. I needed to talk to Zaylen and hear his side of the story. There was three sides to this story; Shauntae's side, Zaylen's side and the truth. And I was not going to sit up here and lie and say that Zaylen had not been there for me through everything, so I at least owe him a chance to explain to me what the fuck is going on with him and Shauntae's crazy ass. So, before I left him, I decided to go and find out what the fuck was going on.

"You know what, ma? I am going to go and talk to him and figure out what is going on. You know you are truly an amazing woman, always dropping knowledge on me." I said while getting up and kissing her on the cheek.

"Tell me something I don't know." She said while smiling and turning to watch her other show *The First 48*. I swear I think that is why my mother is so crazy from watching those damn murder shows.

It wasn't much for me to do to get ready to leave, because I just came straight in and went to sleep. I did want to wash my face and brush my teeth and put my hair up in a high ponytail. Once I took care of my hygiene, I grabbed the keys to my Mama's Audi Q7 and was out the door. I got in the Q7 and fell in love. First of all, the interior was my favorite color red and the leather was soft and it had a sunroof that went all the way to the back. Not to mention how good the sound system was. I was not up on cars and how much they cost, but I know mama paid a nice amount for this truck. I didn't have any money to pay for this if something happens to it. I was actually kind of scared to drive it. I put on Jhene Aiko's *Bullshit* and let the sunroof back and backed out. I swear she be having me all in my feelings. Let me calm my nerves so I could be calm when I made it to the house.

Since we lived on the Eastside, it wasn't nothing for me to hop on 94 and make it downtown to our condo. When I pulled up, I let valet park the truck. I made my way to elevator so that I could go up to our place. For some reason as I was going up the elevator, I started feeling nervous. I had to give myself a pep talk because there was no reason for me to be nervous about shit because I didn't do shit. I mean this will be our first argument in the four years we have been together. I got of the elevator and entered my code to get in when I made it in it was quiet as hell.

"Zaylen," I yelled, I waited on a response, but there was none. So, I went to go look for him he wasn't here. "Where the fuck could he be?" I asked myself out loud. I went to go and grab my phone so that I could call his mother and see if he picked up the truck, but before I could call out, my phone started ringing. It read private on the caller ID. At first, I wasn't going to answer but something in my gut told me to answer it.

"You have a collect call from an inmate at Wayne county jail from Zaylen." The operator said when I picked the phone up.

What the hell is he doing in jail and why is he just now calling me? I hurried up and press one so that I could accept the call. "Hello." I said sounding confused.

"Where the fuck you been Rhae?" Zaylen yelled into the phone like he done lost his damn mind.

"First of all, I was over my mama's house. The question shouldn't be where the fuck was. Why the fuck you in jail?" I yelled back matching his tone.

"Bruh just come fucking get me. You know the safe code. Grab $20,000. I'm downtown in the county. You need to be here ASAP, and I am not fucking playing Rhae." Zaylen said while hanging up the phone. I looked at the phone like it did something to me. I know this nigga didn't just hang up on me like I was the one who put his crazy ass in jail. Since he wanted to act like an ass, he was gon' sit down there for a minute because he was gon' learn I was not his damn child and he better respect me.

I decided to smoke me a joint because a bitch hadn't even been out of jail that long and I got all this damn drama hitting me from all angles. I need to relax my mind before I ended up in the exact place I hated the most fucking; jail. These motherfuckas better leave me alone. I smoked the whole joint and then I went to the safe entered the code and then got the money out so I could bond his ass out. I know his ass better be looking for a new lawyer because I would be damned if his ex bitch represented him.

I made it to the jail in no time due to the fact we lived downtown. Although I was here to pick Zaylen up, I still was scared. Imagine being eighteen and you are in a jail cell facing football numbers! Talking about scared straight, my ass would forever be on the up and up. Fool me once shame on you, fool me twice shame on me. I would never put myself in a position where my freedom is on the line.

I finally made it in the \precinct so I could bail him out.

"I'm here to bail out Zaylen Washington" I said while reaching out in my bag to get the money.

"Okay no problem, but you do know that his bond is $20,000, right?" The CO asked with a raised eyebrow. I wanted to get smart with the heifer, but I decided against it and just pulled out the money and handed it over. She needed to just do her damn job. She looked at me crazy and started the process for Zaylen's release. I decided to go outside and wait because I was becoming claustrophobic sitting in here waiting on his ass.

I got in the truck and started looking through Facebook because I knew it was going to be a minute before they released him. Looking through my timeline it looked like people I went to school with was on the same shit. It was like time stood still. I guess I really didn't miss shit being locked up. I felt like being nosey, so I decided to look on Kazie's page and she still was a rat. Posting all type of damn near nude pictures. I guess she was looking for somebody else's man to fuck with because she can't get her own man.

I never would understand how these bitches are ok with being the side chick. I mean I needed all the attention and you are damn sure ain't gon' be creeping in my damn bed at one or two in the morning and fuck the shit out of me than go home to wifey. Shit I got feelings. Ain't no such thing as fucking with no strings attached in my book because if you fuck with someone, you going to develop feelings for them period.

Shit it was taking forever for them to release Zaylen. I got the munchies and it was some weird people walking around. I made sure the doors were locked and put my seat back to close my eyes for a minute. I didn't even have my eyes closed for five minutes and my phone start ringing. It was Zaylen. He probably was looking for me.

"I'm about to pull up!" I didn't even give
him a chance to respond.

I could see him standing out front looking
mad as hell. I hope he didn't get in here on no
bullshit because nobody had time for that shit today.
I pulled right up in front and unlocked the doors. He
got in and didn't even look at me. Not a 'thanks, bae
for coming to get me,' no kiss, no nothing. One
thing I hated was an ungrateful ass person! I started
to check his ass but decided against it. He was a
whole grown ass man and I know Mrs. Washington
taught him better than that. I was confused as to
why he was even mad at me in the first damn place.

We rode in silence the whole way home.
The shit was pissing me off so bad that by the time
we made it to the condo, I was ready to go to back
to my mom's house. I pulled up to the front and
unlocked the doors so he could get out. I gave his
ass the same energy he was giving me. I didn't even
look at his ass. I was just ready for him to get out so
I could leave. I sat there for a good five minutes and
he still didn't get out.

I finally looked at him and he was just staring at me with his fine ass. I really wanted to hop over the seat and kiss his ass, but this wasn't the right time.

"I'm just trying to figure out where the fuck do you think you about to go?" Zaylen asked while reaching over to hit the button to turn the car off and grabbing the key out of the cup holder.

"Ohhh so you do now how to open your month and talk. If you must know, I'm going back where I am wanted." I yelled while trying to get the key back so I could leave.

"Get the fuck out the car, Rhae and I'm not about to tell you again!" Zaylen said while getting out the car and slamming the door.

This nigga here. I swear to God! The way that he told me to get out of the car gave me chills, so to avoid any confrontation I got my ass out. He still wasn't saying shit to me as we waited on the elevator, so I didn't say shit either. If he wanted to play the silent game, then so be it. Once we made it in the condo, Zaylen started stripping and walking towards the shower.

"Don't be here when I get out this motherfuckin' shower Rhae and it's going to be a motherfuckin' problem. And I promise you, that's not the kind of problem you want to deal with now you can try me if you want to!"

I ain't even going anywhere anyway I thought to myself. I was still trying to figure out why the hell he was so mad at me when I hadn't done anything. He the one who had his ex bitch running me off the road and trying to hit me with an aluminum bat! Fuck this shit. I needed some damn answers and I needed them right now. I burst in the bathroom and all I could do was stare because Zaylen looked so damn delicious right now with that water dripping off his body. Have you ever seen a dick so beautiful it made your mouth water?

"Rhae why you busting through the door like somebody chasing you? I'll be out in a minute." I was still standing there staring. I snapped out of it and just walked back out the door.

I decided to lay down because this shit was irritating my soul. I wish he would just say whatever the fuck he got to say, and we can just move on, because a bitch was horny and needed some dick. I stripped and got my ass in the bed. The silk sheets cooled my hot ass right down.

"I hope you naked under them sheets because after we get done having this discussion, I'm about to get some of my pussy. Now first question. Where you been all fucking day and why the fuck did you have my number blocked? If I were you, I would keep it one thousand because you know I hate a fucking liar!"

"What do you mean where I been all day? I did what hell you asked me to do. I took that paperwork to your mamas."

"So you didn't see my brother at all today?" Zaylen asked while jumping in the bed on top of me.

"Wait what? I didn't see his ass by choice. I guess he was coming to visit your mom and he kidnapped my ass!" Now I know damn well this fool don't think I'm messing around with Za'Kari's ass.

"So why didn't you call me? Let me guess he took your phone too."

"He did take my fucking phone Zaylen. When have I ever lied to you? You think after everything that nigga put me through, I would want anything to do with his dysfunctional ass? How did you find out I was with him?"

"I got eyes everywhere baby trust me."

"Now you fucking lying get the fuck off of me. The only way you knew that was because of your bitch, Shauntae! So while Rhae was locked up everybody was out here doing them. Why would you have your girlfriend represent me and then make me fall in love with you? I would have just been grateful for the help. That's what's wrong with niggas. They always want their cake and eat too. I'm glad I found out before I got pregnant or some shit. You foul just like your brother, and I can't take no more heartache so I'm going to let you and Shauntae be happy just fucking forget about me." I screamed with tears rolling down my face.

I got up and start throwing my shit in bags because I couldn't stand to be in this nigga's presence any longer. I was so mad I didn't realize that every piece of clothing I was packing, Zaylen's ass was unpacking. By the time I realized what he was doing my ass was tired, and I just sat down in the middle of the floor and put my hands on my face.

"Fuck all this shit." I yelled.

Chapter Nineteen

Zaylen

This woman got me so fucked up, thinking I'm just going to let her leave me. I loved Rhae more than life itself and I was going to put a ring on it soon. I wasn't really that mad at her because I know nothing happened. Especially the way Za'Kari was acting when I went to find my baby. I just didn't like the fact that she was anywhere near Za'Kari, I'm very possessive about my woman.

I was also pissed because Za'Kari's bitch ass called the pigs and my ass just had to pay $20,000 just to get out of jail. I was not worried about the charges because I had the best lawyer money could buy and they would be dropped.

"Fuck all what shit, love? Why are you trying to leave me? You know I don't see nobody but you and you know I'm not going to let you leave. We in this shit for the long haul. I've been waiting on your sexy ass for four long years. You think it's just going to be that easy for me to leave you alone? Yes, Shauntae told me that you and my brother were together today, but what you got to know is that nobody can tell me shit about you." I said while getting on my knees in front of her.

"So, you think that shit was cool allowing her to represent me knowing y'all had history? What if the crazy bitch did some shit to make me do more time? And now she even more pissed because she feels played. What if she does some shit to get me put back into jail? That was some snake as shit Zaylen, and you know it. Yeah you helped and I am forever grateful but it's like I'm dealing with the same bullshit again. We not talking about you and me. We're talking about my fucking life." Rhae yelled.

Damn I really didn't think about all the bullshit that could happen once Shauntae found out the truth. I really was just trying to help Rhae and although Shauntae's ass was crazy, she was a damn good attorney. I just needed Rhae to understand that she was fuckin' with a winner. Ain't nothing going to happen to her on my watch and I put that on everything. I know she had trust issues due to all the bullshit my brother put her through, but I was not my brother and it was time that she realized that because I was not going to keep paying for another motherfuckas mistake. I been paying for Za'Kari's mistakes all my damn life that shit has to stop somewhere.

"Look baby, at the time I thought it was cool because me and Shauntae been broke up and I have not been with her for years. I just hired her as my attorney. It was and has been nothing but business. I can't control the next person feelings. Shit, if she can't move on with her life then that's on her. I don't even understand why we are sitting up here talking about her because that shit in the past. I am sitting here telling you that I love you I am madly in love with you and I can't see myself with nobody but you. I am not going to lie, it did something to me when she told me that y'all was together today because I went over Za'Kari's house ready to kill both of y'all and have both of y'all bodies floating in the Detroit river." I said while kissing her on the cheek.

"Oh yeah and none of you motherfuckas heads are wrapped too tight. Why would I even have anything to do with Za'Kari after all the bullshit he did to me from me going to jail and him fucking with my so called best friend? Zaylen, I am not the weak minded little girl you helped four years ago. I am a grown ass woman. Now what you got to know is I am not going to put up with no bullshit from nobody. All these secrets and shit stops today right now. And you better start talking to me like you got some got damn sense. I am your woman, not your child." Rhae said while getting up off the floor.

Fuck! The way she was bossing up and standing up for herself was turning me the fuck on. It was once a time when Rhae would be all timid and crying and weak minded and biting her tongue. But I see she was addressing whatever problems come her way, which surprised the hell out of me. I loved this new Rhae. It was sexy as fuck. I loved women that were bosses and handled their own shit. You can tell she was still mad because she was walking around the room picking up her things and mumbling to herself. I don't know why women did that my mom use to do the same thing when Za'Kari and me was getting on her nerves.

I was just sitting in the middle of the floor watching her walk around the room. I tripped her ass because I was tired of watching her sexy ass walk past me.

"Why the fuck would you trip me Zaylen? What if I would have broken my ankle or some shit?"

"Baby you didn't even fall for real. Your sexy ass fell right into my arms." I said while laughing.

"Zaylen that is not funny!" Rhae said. Before she could get another word out, I kissed her juicy lips. I started off by just pecking her lips, but I wanted more so I slowly inched my tongue into her mouth. I know she was feeling it because she was moaning, and breathing hard. I started kissing her even deeper and her moans became louder, making my dick get even harder. I gently laid her on the floor and started taking all of her clothes off while she stared at me, anticipating what I was about to do next. Rhae smelled so good to me. She smelled like peaches. I could just lick her all over.

Once I had her completely naked, I opened her legs as far as they could go and I dug in, latching on to her clit sucking on it gently. I then stuck my finger inside of her now wet pussy moving in and out while I sucked on her clit. Baby was taking it like a champ. I knew I was doing it right because she was pushing my face deeper and deeper inside of her pussy. I moved my finger and put my tongue inside, going in and out and sucking at the same time. She tasted so good. I was trying to suck her soul out of her. Baby bust the biggest nut and I licked up every drop. Not wanting her to come down off her high, I bent her legs back and inserted all thirteen inches inside her fat, wet pussy. Damn, her shit was so wet. I just knew I was going to nut prematurely. I had to think about some other shit because her pussy was too good just to have a quickie. All you heard in our bedroom was smacking and moaning. I took one of her titties and started sucking on her chocolate nipple. I gently bit it while I stroked her pussy, going deeper and deeper. I wanted to touch her fucking back. I had been waiting so long to feel my baby. At this point, I guess I was going too deep because she was trying to run, but little did she know, that shit was making me go even harder.

"Give me my shit, baby. Why you keep running from your dick?" I asked while still going deeper and deeper.

"Ohhh shit baby you're going deep. Please don't stop!" Rhae moaned in my ear, sounding all sexy and shit.

"Don't worry baby. I'm not, I promise!" I replied while kissing her lips passionately while still stroking. I flipped her over and arched her back in the perfect position. I stroked her from the back, going balls deep. I grabbed her hair as I was stroking and started biting on her neck, leaving passion marks all over her neck marking my motherfuckin' territory. On God, my pussy was magnificent. Thinking about another nigga in this shit had my mind going crazy.

"Baby what you got to know is if you give my pussy away, I am killing you and that nigga. You mine and mine only. You fucking understand me?" I asked while giving her back shots so that she understood. I was not playing with her ass at all.

"Yes, baby. I ain't going nowhere." Rhae moaned.

"That's a good girl," I said while busting the biggest nut I ever had. I made sure every last drop of my semen got up in my pussy. I hoped her ass get pregnant.

Chapter Twenty

Kazie

A Few Weeks Later…

Yeah

Yeah, yeah, yeah, yeah

Hmm, I don't give a fuck

Work, bitch

Fuck you good off a Perc', bitch (Mhm)

Get activated or get hurt, bitch (On God)

If you ain't active, you get murked, bitch

(Ayy)

Go to work, bitch (Ayy)

Twerk, bitch

I walked through the Exhale Hookah Bar like I owned it, rapping along to Sada Baby, a local up and coming Detroit rapper. Sada always had you feeling like you could fuck any nigga or bitch up. And that's exactly how I had been feeling lately. I was getting tired of looking at Rhae and Zaylen all on Facebook in love. Damn, when was I ever going to beat this bitch at this thing called life?

I had been trying to reach out to Shauntae's ass, but she wouldn't return my phone calls or accept my visits when I went to her office. So, I guess I would have to come up with a plan to get Rhae out the picture. Za'Kari didn't call or come by and I already knew he didn't want nothing to happen to his precious Rhae. I walked up to the bar so that I could get me a Patron margarita so I could loosen up a little bit.

After getting my drink, I decided to go sit in the back because I really didn't want anyone to see me. I was only here to make sure my cousin did what the fuck I paid her ass $1000 to do. And that was to put some ketamine in Zaylen's drink and fuck the shit out of him while I recorded him. Hell, I might even jump on the dick for old times sake. I had to laugh at myself because sometimes I could be so damn evil.

I picked up my phone to check the time and realized that it was already eleven. My cousin Toy still hadn't made it here yet. I didn't know why I even bothered asking her slow ass to do anything. I picked up my phone so I could call her and just when I was about to call her, I saw her being patted down by security at the front door. We made eye contact and I raised my glass to let her know it was showtime.

Toy was looking good. If I was a nigga, I would holla at her. She wore a tight red see through Gucci dress that had Gucci all over it and tied up in the back with her back out leaving nothing to the imagination. She had ass for days and her breast were perfect. She didn't even have a bra on, and they were sitting up just right. Her hair was curled to perfection, hanging down her back and her face was naturally to the God's. To complete the look, she had on some red three inch stilettos making her short ass look taller she was just sexy.

I been coming in here for the past few weeks so I could learn Zaylen's routine and just like clockwork, he was behind the bar taking money from the cash register and smoking on Hookah. I watched as Toy approached the bar. I smiled because I knew she would get his attention. She ordered a drink and as she was waiting on the bartender to fix her drink. She was all up in Zaylen's face. Only thing he did was smile and kept doing what he was doing.

The shit was pissing me off because this nigga was not trying to give my cousin the time of day. Ol' loyal ass nigga. I sent her a text message so I could coach her ass because she wasn't trying hard enough.

Me: Bitch, show his ass something make him pay you some attention ask him to have a drink or something damn!

Toy: Bitch what you mean he not giving me the time of day this nigga faithful faithful what the fuck you want me to do?

Me: You better do something or run me my motherfuckin' money tonight!

I know I struck a nerve because it was written all over her face. But I could care less because I needed this shit done tonight. I knew that if she pressed him enough, he would give in because Zaylen didn't like hurting a woman's feelings. He walked around the bar and sat next to her. My heart started racing because my plans were about to fall through.

I saw the bartender put their drinks in front of them. That was my cue to walk up to him and get his attention off of her for a second. I knew I was going to piss him off but oh well.

"What's up Zaylen? Does Rhae know you out here flirting with your customers while you supposed to be working? Let me call her and let her know. I would hate for her to get played again."

"What the fuck are you talking about? This woman knows I'm taken. Ain't shit popping and you know damn well my baby don't fuck with your trifling ass like that! What the fuck you doing in here anyway? I could have sworn I told my security no hoes allowed. Now get the fuck on."

"Damn did I ruffle some feathers? Why you getting so mad if ain't shit going on? But let me get up out of here. I don't want no problems." I said while laughing.

I saw Toy put the drug in his drink. The heifer was slick wit it too. He turned around and downed his drink. His dumb ass was that mad. I winked at her and went to the bathroom. I waited for Toy to meet me in there so that we could sneak into his office, which was right down the hall from the restrooms.

"He just walked to his office. How long you think the drug going to take to start working?" Toy asked.

"Shit I don't know. Not long, I guess. You act like I just give niggas the date rape drug on the regular!"

"Shit I don't know what your evil ass be doing out here. I wouldn't put it passed you." Toy laughed

This bitch had all the jokes, which I didn't see how when she was busting it open for these broke ass niggas. Not trying to waste too much time, I peeked out the bathroom to make sure no one was coming. Once I saw the coast was clear, I motioned for her to follow me. I slowly opened up his office door and walked in and Zaylen had his head down on his desk.

I called his name to see how alert he was. He wasn't alert at all. So, I set my phone up so that it was in the right position so that whoever could see his face clearly. While I was setting the phone up, I told Toy to go ahead and start undressing him. When I turned around, I had to control my damn hormones. Zaylen's body was banging. The man had a six pack that made you want to lick every single muscle and let's not talk about the size of his dick. It looked hard even though it was soft. Now how is that even possible? Shit Toy's ass didn't waste no time getting started. She got down on her knees and started stroking his dick. It didn't take much for it to get hard. She then started giving him head, moving her head up and down. She must have being doing a good job because he began moaning and grabbing her head guiding her on how to give him head the way he liked.

"Shit Rhae baby. Damn you must have really missed daddy! Ohh shit just like that baby."

Damn this nigga was drugged, and he was still thinking about Rhae's ass. I stood off to the side watching Toy do her thing on this nigga. All I could think about was the look on Rhae's face when she saw the video. I knew her little heart is going to be broken. Good maybe her ass would come down off that high horse she was on.

Toy was looking like a real porn star right now. She was taking the dick like a champ. After they both bust their nuts, I ended the recording. That session was so good I wanted to hop on the dick my damn self. But I didn't want to get caught back here with Zaylen because the Hookah Bar was about to close, so I just waited for Toy to get cleaned up so we could get the hell up out of here.

Toy walked out the bathroom with a smirk on her face.

"Yeah that dick was definitely worth every penny you gave me. Matter of fact, when his bitch leaves his ass, I'll be more than happy to take his ass off her hands. Whew chile."

"Bitch come on. We got to go. We don't have time to be sitting up here reminiscing and shit. Because if he wakes up, neither one of our asses would live to see another day!"

I peeked out the door first to make sure the coast was clear and it was, so I grabbed Toy by the arm and ran out the door and out the bar. I didn't breathe until I made it out the door. Lord knows I was so scared. Toy and I got into separate cars and left. I couldn't wait to get home so I could send Rhae this video. *Mission accomplished* I thought to myself. If you want shit done, you had to do it your damn self.

Chapter Twenty-One

Rhae

I was so excited because I was finally able to get an appointment to take my test so I could drive around legally. With all this Covid shit going on, you couldn't do anything. I mean it wasn't like it really mattered anyway. Probably fifty percent of Detroit drove around illegally. I just don't want to give the pigs no reason to take me back to that hell hole.

I pulled into the parking lot of the DMV on Grand Blvd on the west side and got out. I made sure to lock the doors because if I didn't, I could guarantee that Zaylen's truck would not be out here when I came back out. I walked in and stood in the appointment line so that I could get the test. As I was standing in line, I heard Za'Kari's voice. I started to walk right back out the door, but I couldn't do that because if I missed my appointment, it would be months before I could get another one.

So, I just stood behind him praying that he didn't see me because I really didn't feel like dealing with his pathetic ass. I stood in line scrolling Instagram to pass time while waiting on my number to be called.

"Number 189," the customer service rep yelled, while looking around to see who had the number. At first, I hesitated because she was right next to the old man who was helping Za'Kari.

Next thing I know she had called the next number.

"Number 190."

"Whew, the devil is really trying me today," I said out loud. I politely took my number 189 and walked my ass right up to the counter. "Umm excuse me, love, but I am 189. You didn't give me a chance to get up here."

"I did give you plenty of time. You were looking dead at me. Are you hard of hearing?" The girl asked me while raising her eyebrow.

Just when I was about to check her ass, here came Za'Kari's dramatic ass.

"Bitch, are you crazy? Who the fuck are you talking to like that? Matter of fact, where is the manager around this motherfucka because I'll be damned if I let some random ass broad talk to my fiancé like that. Actually, you're dismissed. Go help the next motherfucka because you don't even deserve to breathe the same air as my baby! Now did you hear that or are you motherfuckin' hard of hearing?"

I wanted to laugh because poor little tink tink looked like she wanted to cry, but I didn't want Za'Kari to think that I was impressed about the little scene he just made. So, I just turned around and started walking towards the door because at this point, I was over the whole day. The shit was embarrassing all I wanted to do was take my damn driver's test.

Of course, before I could make it to the truck, Za'Kari was on my heels.

"Rhae baby where are you going? I know you are not about to let that ugly broad waste your time. What did you come here for anyway?" Za'Kari asked while grabbing my arm to slow me down from walking so fast. I snatched my arm away from him because I didn't want him touching me at all.

"Not today Za'Kari. You always have to be over the top with shit. I can fight my own battles. I am a grown ass woman, and I can take of myself. Stop following me. Stop stalking my Facebook and Instagram page. Stop riding past my mom's house. Just leave me the fuck alone. What part of I don't like you and I most definitely don't want your ass don't you understand? I am with Zaylen and I am not about to fuck up with him for you or nobody else. You want to know why I am so loyal to my man? It's because when I was locked up like an animal in a cage for some shit, I didn't do he was there. He made sure I had money on my books. I received a letter from him every week! He didn't miss not one visit and he made sure my mama and sisters were straight! Let's not even talk about how he respects me. He puts me first and encourages me to pursue my dreams and he would never have me into no shit that would get me locked up. How many times did you put your hands on me? How many times did you call me out of my name? What about cheating on me with my so-called best friend? You think I want to be with someone like you? Yeah I know motherfuckas change, but ain't no coming back from the shit you put me through. I am supposed to be walking across Jackson State University stage getting my degree in Business Management not standing here at the DMV trying to get my driver's license for the first time. The best thing you can do for me is to leave me alone and stay the fuck out of my life. I swear to God you keep tempting me to put a bullet in your head and go to jail for something I did fucking do." I didn't even give him a chance to respond I just got in the truck and pulled off.

Once I got far away from him and I knew he wasn't following me, I pulled into the CVS parking lot and parked. I just sat in the car crying my eyes out. I didn't really talk about it but going to jail really did something to me. I felt like a failure. I felt betrayed and I had trust issues. I found myself lurking through Zaylen's phone and stalking his Facebook and Instagram pages to see if I see any hoes trying to get at him. I let one nigga fuck up my whole life because I was in love with him and he didn't give a fuck about me. My phone started ringing and it was Zaylen calling. I tried to get myself together because he would know something was wrong just by the tone of my voice.

"Hey, baby. What's up?"

"What's wrong love? Where are you?"

"Nothing is wrong Zay. What are you talking about? Why did you ask me that?" He hung up on me so fast I couldn't even get the rest of my sentence out. Before I knew it, my phone was ringing again with a FaceTime call.

I answered looking into the camera smiling because this man loved me so much and it felt damn good to have a good man. I was going to work on trusting him and stop making him pay for another man's fuck up.

"Now what's wrong love? Why do it look like you been crying? Who do I have to fuck up?" Zaylen asked while putting on his shoes.

"Zay where you going? Baby I am fine. I was just frustrated because the lady at the DMV pissed me off talking about I didn't have an appointment and I had to reschedule my appointment. I am on my way home."

"Oh okay because you know I don't fuck around about you. But I was calling you to let you know we are leaving tonight. I got a surprise for you. Don't worry about packing because you don't need to. I am hungry though and I ain't talking about no food either, so hurry up. I'll be laying in this big ass bed with my tongue out waiting on you to come and sit on daddy's face."

"Shit if that's the case, I'll be there in a few minutes daddy," I said while putting my seatbelt on and pulling off.

I wondered what surprise he had for me. Zaylen was always doing something for me. I couldn't wait until I get myself together so I could return the favor. I did enroll in Wayne State University and I started school in January. Now the only thing that I had to do is find a job. That was going to be hard because everybody always wanted to hire someone who had experience, but how could you get experience if no one would hire you? I was not going to worry about that right now. The only thing I was worried about right now is what my man had in store for me. I was not even going to tell him about my little encounter with Za'Kari today, because I already knew what the outcome is going to be. My phone started ringing again, but this time it was a private caller. I answered but all they were doing was breathing on the phone. I knew it was Za'Kari's ass. That's exactly why I kept my location off so that he couldn't ping my location. I just hung up and turned the music up.

I wanted to make one more stop before I went home and that was to check on my mama and my little sisters. Since I have been out, I had been trying to be a good role model for my little babies, because this world was way different then it was when I was their age. There was sex trafficking and all type of crazy shit going on. I wanted them to know that there was more to life then what these Detroit streets were offering. When I pulled on my mama's block, there was police and fire trucks everywhere. I wondered what the hell going on over here. It gave me a flashback of when they ran up in my house. I shook that thought off and tried to find somewhere to park. Oh my God it looked like they were at my mama's house. I got out and started running towards my mother's house. It looked like her house was on fire. Before I could make it to their house, Peaches ran up to me crying.

"Peaches baby what happened? Where is mama and Passion?" I asked while looking her over to make sure that she was okay,

"Rhae somebody threw something in the window and our house caught on fire. Who would do that?" Peaches asked while crying. I knew she was scared and upset, but she was not giving me the information I needed. I needed to know where my mama and my other little sister were. I grabbed her by the hand and started walking towards the house.

Then I saw the ambulance bringing my mama out the house on a stretcher. If I wouldn't have saw her eyes opened, I probably would have lost it. There was blood everywhere and I had no clue where the blood was coming from because they had her covered up. Right behind her they were bringing out my baby sister Passion out on the stretcher, but she was unconscious, and they were giving her oxygen.

"What the hell happened." I yelled. I looked around and all the nosey ass neighbors were looking at me like I was crazy. "One of you nosey motherfuckas saw something. What the hell happened?" I yelled again.

"Rhae come on. We got to go to the hospital with mama and Passion!" Peaches yelled while pulling me to the truck. I ran and jumped in the truck so I could follow the ambulances to the hospital. As I was trying to keep up with the ambulances, my mind was everywhere. I couldn't believe somebody threw a fucking bomb through my mama's window.

We don't beef with nobody and everybody in my neighborhood loved my mama. My phone started ringing again and I already knew it was Zaylen. I was supposed to have been at home.

"Zay meet me at St. John's hospital. Please don't ask me no questions right now. baby. Just meet me there." I hung up because I didn't want to be on my phone while I was driving crazy. We pulled in the hospital and I parked right behind the ambulance. I didn't give a fuck about being parked illegally. They could tow the motherfucka if they wanted to. I needed to see what was going on with my mama and little sister.

We ran in the door but before I could make it into the hospital, the security stopped us.

"Are you coming here to be treated Ma'am?"

"Ah no that was our mom and sister who just came in here by ambulance and I need to get in there to see what's going on?" I answered becoming more and more frustrated.

"I'm sorry ma'am but you can't go in due to Covid. What's your contact information so that the doctor can call you once they figure out what's going on?"

I looked at the security guard like he lost his damn mind. I didn't understand why I couldn't go and see what the hell going on with my fucking family. I wanted to spazz out but that wasn't going to get me back there to my mama, so I gave the security my information and grabbed my sister Peaches hand and walked back out the doors.

"That some bullshit Rhae. We need to see what's going on with ma and Passion." Peaches said with tears running down her face.

At this moment, I felt fucking helpless. I didn't know what was going on and I had no fucking clue who threw a fucking bomb through my mama's window. As we were walking back to the truck, we heard some tires screeching. I looked over and it was Zaylen. He hopped out his Audi and ran over to me and started looking me all over.

"Zay it's not me. It's my mama and Passion."

"What the fuck happened to mama and Lil P, baby?"

"I don't know somebody threw a fucking bomb through the window."

"What the hell you mean somebody threw a bomb through the window? Mama B don't beef with nobody and I know Lil P and Peaches not into no drama so I'm clueless. Nobody saw who did it? Somebody got to know something and why y'all standing out here and not in there seeing what's going on?" Zaylen said while pointing towards the hospital.

"They won't let us in due to Covid, baby. Mama wasn't looking too good when I saw her. I don't know what I am going to do if I lose my mama or my baby sister. I just got them back!" I said while hugging him.

"Mama B is not going nowhere. She still got some shit to fuck up in this world and so does Lil P.

Go and park the truck and wait there while I make some phone calls. I need to find out what the fuck happened! Don't you worry about shit baby. Let me take care of everything from here. I think motherfuckas forgot who the fuck I am." Zay said while kissing my lips.

I didn't even have the strength to argue about going to the truck because I was beyond tired, both physically and mentally. I motioned for Peaches to follow me so that I could park the truck and play the waiting game. I parked and began to pray. I know that you were not supposed to question God, but I didn't understand why he had allowed all of the bullshit to happen to me.

Chapter Twenty-Two

Damn if you want something done you have to do it your damn self. I paid this idiot $20,000 to kill the bitch Rhae and he paid a damn crack head to throw a bomb through her mother's window and she wasn't even there! Who the hell does that? He could have ran the bitch off the road or shot her ass in the head. Here I was watching my man consoling the motherfucka I wanted dead.

Now I done created more problems for my damn self because if Zaylen found out that I had something to do with this shit, I was going to have hell to pay. The only thing I knew left to do was call Za'Kari's ass and I didn't really want to do that because I already knew that he was going to talk shit. I took a deep breath and picked my phone up to call his irritating ass.

"What's up Shauntae?"

"I need your help. I think I fucked up bad!"

"Okay and what the fuck you calling me for? What do you want me to do about it?"

This is exactly why I didn't want to call him in the first damn place. He always got a fucked up attitude.

"Look I paid JT to do something to that heifer Rhae and this idiot turns around and pays someone else to do his dirty work. The idiot he hired threw a damn firebomb through her mother's window while she wasn't there. Only her mom and little sisters were there, and now I'm scared that Zaylen will find out."

"You did what? Why the hell would you do some dumb shit like that? I thought I told you that nothing happens to Rhae!!! You better be lucky I am not in front of you right now because if I was, I would slap fire from your dumb ass. You know damn well that Zaylen don't play about Rhae. He didn't play about you when y'all was together. And then you go and hire JT's crazy ass. Oh yeah you in trouble. You know all anybody has to do is wave money in front of his face and he's running off at the mouth. You should have called me first before you made a move like that! So, since you made that dumb ass decision on your own, you figure out how to get out this shit on your own!" Za'Kari said while hanging up.

I looked at the phone, because I just knew Za'Kari didn't just hang up on me. That was exactly why I should have gone with my first mind and not called his ass at all, because he just added more stress to my stressful life. I was not going to worry about none of this shit right now. I was about to go home roll me up a fat ass joint and take me a double shot of Patron. I had never been so happy to be at home in my life. I parked my Range and got out and set my alarm. I was speed walking to my door because even though it was only six, it was still dark as hell outside due to time going back. I unlocked the door and walked in and turned on my hallway light and dropped my brief case by the front door.

I was so stressed that the first thing I did was head toward my bar so that I could get a double shot of Patron. I turned on the light so I could see and I almost had a heart attack because Zaylen was sitting on my couch.

"Hey Zay what are you doing sitting in my house in the dark?" I asked while try to catch my breath.

He didn't say anything. The only thing he did was just sit there and stare at me with a psychotic look in his eyes. As he was looking at me, I was planning my escape. The way he was looking at me right now, it looked like he could snap my neck. If didn't nobody else know me Zaylen did and he knew when I was lying. That's why I was trying not to talk at all. The longer he stared at me, the more scared I became. Shit I left my phone on the counter so there was no way that I could call 911. He finally cleared his throat, and I was just waiting to hear what was about to come out of his mouth.

"So, where you been all day Shauntae and make sure you answer honestly because you know I know when you are fucking lying."

"I been in court all day. Why are you checking me like I did something wrong?"

"Humph court all day huh? Did you know that somebody threw a fucking bomb through my wife's mother's house? Now you wouldn't have anything to do with that now would you?" Zaylen asked me.

"Wife? When did you get fucking married? Why would I have that bitch's mother house bombed? Don't you think I would have just had her killed!" I yelled.

When those last words came out of my mouth, I swear to God I wanted to take them back or say I was just playing or something. Before I could even begin to apologize, Zaylen choked slammed me to the ground and still had his hand around my throat.

"What the fuck did you just say because I can't hear you. You would have had who killed?" I was grabbing and scratching this psycho's hands so that he could let me go because I felt like I was about to pass out at any moment. How do you ask a question and then expect someone to answer when you have your hands around their throat? I guess he saw me about to lose conscious, so he let me go. "I think you're fucking lying. You want to know why? Because you are a vindictive little bitch who thinks the world revolves around you. You think that everything is supposed to go your way, but it doesn't. You know my girl's mother Brenda and little sister Passion died. They are gone. They are not coming back. And for what? Because a selfish bitch can't accept rejection. I don't know for sure that you had something to do with it, but this is my fucking city and I am about to make the streets bleed until I find out who the fuck did it. So, if it was you that had something to do with it, just know I am coming for your ass and I am going to kill you. You know how the fuck I ride for mine. Right now, I am going to go home and support my baby because she is going through hell. If I were you, I would get the fuck up out of the D like yesterday." He left me in the middle of the floor still trying to catch my breath.

Once I was able to catch my breath, I got up and started pacing the floor. What the hell was I going to do? The only thing I could think of was to get to JT before anyone else did and kill his ass. My only problem was that I have no clue where the hell to find him at. I went into my room so that I could get out of my work clothes because time was not on my side. I found me some black leggings and a black hoodie with my black timbs, I pulled my hair up into a high ponytail. I went to my safe and grabbed my 9 mm. I went to my garage and pulled out my little shooter I used when I was up to no good. I called JT's phone and he answered on the first ring.

"You got another job for me already?"

"Yeah I do. Where can you meet me at?" I asked while backing out the driveway.

"Meet me at Nicky D's on 6mile and Livernois."

"Okay give me about thirty minutes." I replied while hanging up the phone.

Damn I should have used my other phone. Oh well I was going to dump his ass somewhere where he could never be found, and no one really liked his snitching ass anyway. I hopped on 75 so that I could get off at Davison Freeway. I was glad that all that construction was over. I pulled up in front of Nicky D's and it was nowhere to park as usual, so I parked in the alley. I called JT to let him know I was outside. While I was waiting, I screwed my silencer on because I wasn't going to waste no time. I was going to kill his ass as soon as he got in the car. He came out and came to the passenger side door and got in.

"What's up? You know this is your second favor I am doing. It's going to cost you a lot more, but you're big money. You got it. Plus you don't want to get those pretty little hands dirty." JT said while laughing. I didn't respond. I just cocked my nine and put it to his head and pulled the trigger. It was blood everywhere I knew I had to take his body it and dump it, but I couldn't drive around with blood all on the inside. I got out so that I could get my cleaning supplies out the trunk and just my fucking luck, the pigs were flashing their lights on me!

FUCK! FUCK! FUCK !!!

To Be Continued…

A Message from the Author

Hi, Readers!

I hope that you enjoyed reading this book as much I enjoyed writing it. I know I haven't dropped a book in a long time. But when you are going through things in life, it is pretty hard to stay focus and write. I want to thank a few people for always encouraging me to keep pushing. my Niece Tanjanika Lane. My friend my mentor and one of the dopest author's in the Literary world, Shalaine Powell, I really do appreciate you rocking with me when I had other people that doubted me. To my best friend in the whole wide world, Jessica Reynolds. Thanks for always believing in me and continuing to push me to be the best I love you woman it's nowhere but up from here baby. To my siblings Dawana Frye, Torson Williams, and Ronnie Jenkins Jr. you know how I feel about y'all. If you rocking, I am rolling. Jerusha Wright, thank you for being your crazy self and uplifting me when I was down. Finally, to my son, Da'karri Rashawn

Jenkins. I love you more than life itself. You are my strength when I am weak. You are my motivation and you are the reason why I do what I do.

If you are a reader and would like to get in contact with me, I can be reached on Facebook Roshonda Jenkins

Instagram Authoress_Ro J

Email Roshondajenkins@gmail.com

If you are a reader, please leave a review it would be greatly appreciated! I hope you are ready for Part 2 because it's dropping soon. Authoress Ro J is bacccccck!